The Messenger

K. M. Deal

Aberdeen Bay

Harbin - Washington, D.C. - San Diego

Aberdeen Bay
Published by Aberdeen Bay, an imprint of Champion Writers.
www.aberdeenbay.com

PUBLISHER'S NOTE

This is a book of fiction. Names, characters, places, and
incidents are either the product of author's imagination or are
used fictitiously. Any resemblance to actual persons, living or
dead, business establishments, government agencies, events,
or locales is entirely coincidental.

International Standard Book Number
ISBN-13: 978-1-60830-070-9
ISBN-10: 1-60830-070-6

Printed in the United States of America.

To Phillip, my husband and best friend

Acknowledgments

I am forever indebted to the following people for their contributions to this book:

To: the wonderful team at Aberdeen Bay, including Ross Murphy and Andy Zhang, who gave me the chance.

To: the Hillside Book Club and my first readers, Peggy Altherr, Gale Blevins, Jeanelle and Nick Brown, Maureen Lok, Jody Thurber, and Ronald Deal (who is also my brother-in-law).

To: all my family for their love and support.

And finally to my husband, Phillip, my love and greatest champion.

Prologue

Decatur, GA
September, 2010

Mourners circle a gravesite and huddle in clusters beneath their black umbrellas. An ancient oak looms over them, its gnarled limbs backlit by a glowering sky. It is the perfect day for a funeral in the perfect historic cemetery in Decatur, GA.

The man stands alone on a hilltop, too far away to see details. His dark eyes scan the Mercedes-Benzes, BMWs, and Lexuses lining the narrow road to the gravesite, then snap back to the scene playing out before him. He cups his hands, lights a cigarette, and squints against the cold drizzle blown horizontal by the wind. The smoke fills his lungs, drifts to his head and releases the tension in his body. *God is good.* The full lips curve slightly.

Yes, infidels, it is fitting that you mourn. This is only the beginning.

Chapter One

Ramallah, West Bank of Israel
July, 2010

The afternoon sun slanted across the marketplace. Kamal Nasser did not want to be there. He was deaf to the familiar sounds of vendors hawking their wares, children shouting at play, and cars clattering and honking through the narrow streets. He ignored the smells of baking bread, rotting vegetables, urine, and spices. A brass pot of cardamom-laced Turkish coffee sat in front of him. An ancient olive tree stretched knotty limbs to provide welcome shade over the table. Still, beads of sweat were forming on the crest of his upper lip. Kamal did not want to be here sitting across from this man.

He introduced himself as *Al Ustadh*, a term of respect for teacher or professor. Kamal did not know the man's name and had no desire to learn it. He watched in silence as The Teacher, being careful not to disturb the sediment at the bottom of the pot, poured two small cups of steaming coffee. His brown hands were graceful with long tapering fingers. The two men raised their cups at the same time, "*Alhumdulillah* (praise God)," they saluted.

Smiling, The Teacher proffered a pack of Marlboro Lights. Kamal's hands shook as he pulled a cigarette from the pack. The man struck a match and cupped it with his left hand. Hesitating a moment, Kamal leaned forward towards the flame. The man across from him nodded and smiled again, but his eyes were flat and dead as the darkest pit of hell. American cigarettes were a luxury, but Kamal tasted only ashes. He cursed himself for being a fool. But it was too late.

"So, tell me about your brother in America, the doctor." Settling back in his chair, The Teacher steepled his fingers and raised an inquiring eyebrow.

Chapter Two

Decatur, GA
August, 2010

"Sameeee! The party is starting." Karen's voice, bouncing off yellow plaster walls and aged oak floors, echoed down the long hallway.

Dr. Sami Nasser grunted as he completed a paragraph on the report he was typing and clicked 'Save'. He was excited about the new Global Health Fellowship program with the Centers for Disease Control (CDC). As a neurologist and researcher at Emory University, he welcomed the opportunity to work with leading epidemiologists on global medical concerns. Working on priority health conditions in conjunction with CDC staff, students would spend six to twelve weeks in a developing country. He wished he'd had the opportunity when he was a medical student.

"I've become soft," Sami thought. Leaning back, he stretched the stiff muscles in his shoulders as he scanned the study. Cherry paneling gleamed on the walls, and books nestled in the built-in shelves across from him. A well-worn section of medical volumes and journals dominated, but was flanked by philosophy, history, literature, and a significant number of books in Arabic. The jewel-colored *Bijar*, thick and luxuriant, rested beneath his feet. Called the Iron rug of Persia, the densely packed pile produced a cushioned effect that was matched by few other rugs. This was his room, his sanctum sanctorum, and it was a far cry from a field tent in the third world.

Rising from his chair, he collected a pile of papers and dumped them in a desk drawer. Leaving the solitude of his study, Sami followed party sounds to the kitchen. He paused at the entrance to watch his wife rummaging through the junk drawer. Her tight black jeans presented a nice rear view.

"It's about time!" Karen exclaimed as she turned to see him framed in the doorway. "Honey do you have any matches?" She brushed a lock of hair behind her ear.

Smiling, he pulled a battered Zippo out of his pocket and waved it in front of her nose. Shaking her head, Karen held out her hand. "Why do you carry this thing around? You haven't smoked for years."

Sami raised his dark brows and shrugged. "Habit. Now where is my beautiful birthday girl?"

"I'm here Daddy!" Five-year old Mira Nasser was balanced on her knees, bouncing in her chair. "Wait till you see the cake mommy bought!" Flanking his daughter was a ring of giggling, pastel-clad little girls. Sunlight from the bay window speckled the wall behind them. With her black hair and creamy skin, Mira looked like a princess from the Arabian Nights.

A ripple of "ooooohs" made its way around the table as Karen set the cake down in front of her daughter. Sami grimaced at the lavender tinged frosting and the pink and yellow Barbie adorning the center of the cake.

"Everybody be quiet now," Mira commanded. "My daddy is going to sing Happy Birthday to me in Arabic."

Sami took a seat across from his daughter. His eyes never left her face as he sang.

Sena helwa ya jamila,
Sena helwa ya jamila,

The flickering candle flames reflected in her huge brown eyes.

Sena helwa ya Mira,
Sena helwa ya jamila.

"Now make a wish and blow out the candles, baby," said Karen.

"But what should I wish for?" Mira asked, turning a pleading gaze on her parents.

"Wish for anything in the whole world, *habibti*," her father answered. The little girl closed her eyes and scrunched up her face. Then taking a deep breath, she opened her eyes and blew out the five purple-striped candles.

Scooping ice cream at the kitchen counter, Sami watched his wife pass along slices of cake, while she sorted out who wanted strawberry ice cream and who wanted vanilla. The volume was rising as Karen sought to fairly distribute icing flowers and chunks of Barbie. A little redhead was clamoring for chocolate.

"I told you there is no chocolate," piped Mira. "Everything has to be pink and purple because those are my favorite colors and today is *my* birthday."

Sami smiled. The pink and purple streamers and balloons did indeed overwhelm the muted earth tones of the kitchen. Mira sounded just like his mother, her namesake. His daughter was not about to put up with any crap. He vowed she would never have to if he could help it.

"Girls, you need to eat your ice cream before it melts." Karen had turned on her teacher voice. "No swimming until everyone finishes her cake." This brought a fresh round of squeals as little mouths were crammed with sugar and cream.

"I'm done," chirped the redhead, pushing away her plate and sliding out of her chair. "Me too! Me too!" Chairs scraped across the tile floor, and eight little bodies scrambled towards the back stairs.

Karen dropped the bowl she was washing in the sink. "Girls? Girls! Listen to me! I want each one of you to wash your hands in the bathroom before you touch anything. Understand? You can change into your suits in Mira's room."

She smiled at the chorus of "Yes ma'ams!" and rolled her eyes, as she pictured the destruction of her powder room.

After dumping the last of the soggy paper plates in the trash, Sami came up behind his wife and circled her waist with his hands. "You are a good mother," he said in her ear.

"You're a good father." She leaned back against his solid frame so that her head rested just under his chin, and he could smell her hair. "Mira was very proud of you today. So was I."

"Hmph! Wish our neighbors were so accommodating." Karen felt him stiffen and drop his hands from her hips.

"Sami don't. Not today." She turned to face him and put a soapy hand to his cheek. "You're being too sensitive. Like my dad said, the world is different now."

"Really? How many children did you invite to Mira's party? Twelve? Thirteen?"

"You don't know for sure why the others didn't come."

"Give it up Karen. We both know why they didn't come. For the same reason the old fart next door runs back in his house when I say good morning." Sami leaned over the sink and glowered through the window at the neighboring yard. "Thinks I'm going to plant a bomb up his shriveled ass."

"Shhhh! The kids are coming down." Karen's lips twitched but she tried to look disapproving. "That is not very charitable."

Sami smiled. "I'll leave charity to you Christians."

Mira burst into the room clad in a pink dotted two-piece swimsuit with a ruffle around the bottom. She'd picked up on the last part of her parents' conversation. "Papa and Nana are Christians, aren't they?"

"Yes sweetie, they are," Karen answered.

"Are they coming tonight for dinner?" Am I really getting another birthday cake?"

"Yes they are, and yes you are. I'm starting a grown-up cake right now." Karen plopped a dab of flour on her daughter's upturned nose.

"Mommy!" the little girl giggled and rubbed at the

white smudge. "Now I'll have to wash it off in the pool."

"You wait until an adult is with you," Karen warned, looking over Mira's head at her husband. "Can you honey? Just till I finish in the kitchen."

"Karen I've got reports to finish," Sami complained, but his daughter had already grabbed his arm and was jumping up and down.

"Yes Daddy, please! Please! You can throw us in the water!" Two dark pigtails bobbed up and down, brushing her tanned shoulders. A few wispy curls escaped to frame the small upturned face. Her cheekbones were already prominent, like her mother's.

Sami sighed, allowing his daughter to drag him through the French doors to the backyard pool. "You owe me for this," he called over his shoulder. "I intend to collect later."

Karen raised a suggestive eyebrow. She watched them through the window. The yard was resplendent with the last breath of summer. The swimming pool shimmered like an aquamarine set in a nest of impatiens and ferns. Several huge magnolias served as a backdrop, their dusky leaves set off by a final showing of snowy blooms. A tangle of honeysuckle crept across the lattice covering the terrace. High-pitched whoops and shrieks cut through the humid air as the little girls splashed and swam, and Sami tried in vain to keep dry.

Karen smiled. She was a lucky woman, and she knew it.

Chapter Three

Decatur, GA

Running fingers through his thick black hair, Sami closed his eyes, opened them and refocused on the computer screen in front of him. He scanned the article sent to him by Moussa Hayek, a friend and epidemiologist from the CDC. It touted the newly appointed director as the first woman to be appointed to the position. She was praised as a champion of global warming research, and rumors abounded that she planned to reduce the focus on bioterrorism.

Sami was appalled by the political pandering. Ideologies of any kind should not influence science. Unfortunately, the real world intervened. The usual suspects aligned themselves with their parties and expressed outrage at supposedly watered-down or trumped-up research—as if they could recognize a scientific study if it slapped them in the face. Politics, as usual, trumped everything.

He wondered how this might affect his own fellowship program. Brooding over the far reaching tentacles of political correctness, he contemplated a decanter of single malt on the shelf in his study. The glow from his desk lamp glittered on the vessel's crystal facets and ignited the amber liquid within.

His attention was diverted when his office phone rang. He glanced at the Caller ID which displayed "Out of Area", and this annoyed him. He pushed the speaker phone button and prepared himself for some telemarketer's screed.

"*As-salaamu aleikum* (Peace be with you)." The voice reverberated in the silence of the incubated room. Its accent was

Egyptian. The disembodied caller continued in formal Arabic. "I bring greetings from your family and your homeland. A messenger awaits you. You will be contacted soon, *Inshallah* (If God wills)."

Sami snatched up the receiver but heard only the distinctive click of disconnection. He recorded all calls on his work phone, so he could refer back to details, if needed. Now he jabbed the button to replay the call. He listened intently and then played the call again.

Was this a prank? His instincts told him no. He wondered if he had been randomly selected or if his family back in Ramallah was involved. Up until now, they had remained apolitical to his knowledge. As educated Muslims living in the occupied territory, the luxury of remaining neutral was possibly no longer an option. He feared this during his last visit home two years ago.

Prior to that, Sami had not been home since 2001. The change during those seven years was phenomenal. Astonished by the Western-style coffee shops and bars, he noticed the English slang peppering Arabic conversations. Men and women chatted openly, some sipping beer despite the Islamic prohibition on alcohol. The upscale restaurants and nightclubs attracted Americans, Israelis, and Europeans. Sprouting embassies reinforced the feeling that Ramallah would become the internationally recognized capital of Palestine.

But factions existed that resented the abandoning of Jerusalem in favor of Ramallah. They accused the Palestinian Authority, formed in 1994 to govern parts of the West Bank and Gaza Strip, of being in collusion with Israel. Despite the booming economic and cultural growth, an undercurrent of violence was always present, as if the city existed in a bubble that could burst at any moment.

His parents had enjoyed a visit to the United States when Mira was a baby, and Sami had pressed them to emigrate. They refused, and he understood their feelings though he feared for them. He feared even more for his younger brother, Kamal. Dropping his face into his hands, Sami thought of his parents.

Chapter Four

Ramallah, West Bank of Israel
1973

Nabil Nasser married his bride Amira late in life. They met at Birzeit College, later to become Birzeit University, where both were teachers. Photos of Nabil taken in his youth showed him as tall and strikingly handsome, looking much like Sami. But the photos did not show his club foot, which marked him as tainted in a culture that viewed physical affliction as a sign of Allah's displeasure.

Barred from most physical games and the camaraderie of boys his age, Nabil poured all his energy into his studies and music. He excelled at math and was a natural musician playing both the violin and the Middle Eastern lute called an *oud*. Though a bachelor, he was much in demand for local weddings where he sang the old folk songs in a pure and vibrant voice as his nimble fingers plucked out melodies in their complex rhythmic structure.

Nabil's father owned several shops in Ramallah. A successful businessman, he valued education and innovation. Fortunately Nabil's elder brother followed in his father's footsteps which left Nabil free to pursue a doctorate degree in statistics. He found his calling as a professor. His music and his duties at the college dominated his life and compensated for his physical affliction.

At Birzeit, his colleagues viewed the middle-aged statistics professor as an aloof, almost stern man. Amira found him attractive with his fine features and thick dark hair sprinkled with gray. But she had never seen him smile, until one evening when she watched him perform at a cousin's wedding. Years later, she often related the story to her sons—outside of their father's hearing, of course.

Amira was small, dark and wiry with flashing black eyes that dominated her otherwise unremarkable face. The youngest of four sisters, she was the most inquisitive and intelligent. Amira's father was a successful merchant though his grandmother, Salima, was born a Bedouin. As a child, she roamed the borders of Jordan with her tribe, but over the years the members became increasingly settled in the villages and cities. In her old age, she was taken in by her grandson, Suliman, who was the son of her eldest son and Amira's father.

From the first, Amira and her great grandmother formed a bond that spanned the generations. When not in school, the little girl spent her free hours at the old woman's side. She delighted in tending to her grandmother's needs, doling out medications and reciting from her lesson books. Amira's parents and sisters were mystified but relieved that *Site* (grandmother) was cared for so cheerfully. All felt it was their duty, but for Amira it was her pleasure.

Site's face had been burned brown from eight decades under the desert sun and was dry as a withered leaf. But the blue tribal tattoos still showed in the wrinkles on her upper lip and on her forehead. A film marred her once beautiful eyes, and she appeared to gaze into some far off world, especially when her great-grand daughter sat at her feet and listened with rapt attention to stories of the desert. She wanted the child to understand her heritage which blazed with tales of courage and honor and was peopled with beautiful women and fierce warriors. It was a dying world that could only live on in the children and their children.

When she finished high school, Amira begged her father to let her study at the prestigious Birzeit College. Teachers invited to their home for tea and sweets broached the subject but were quickly discharged by the head of the household. Two of Amira's sisters were already married, and Suliman was adamantly opposed to the idea of his daughter attending a school with men. Only after months of Site haranguing him to the point of distraction, did he throw up his hands and agree, adding a stern warning of dire consequences should his name be dishonored.

Three months after entering the University, Amira's beloved Site died in her sleep. The girl was inconsolable and withdrew into her studies. Fiercely determined to excel as a tribute to her great-grandmother, she shut out all frivolous past times and acquaintances. Her reputation as a scholar with a quick tongue warded off male suitors, as did her direct attitude. Amira saved her smiles and mischief for her nephews and nieces whom she adored, and she became universally known as *Amti*.

Amira was thirty-three when she attended the wedding that would change her life. She sat back in the shadows of an arbor and watched the young people dance while the old women clapped and trilled in the ancient Bedouin way. Her eyes locked on the face of one man transfigured with joy, as his long fingers cajoled the heavenly notes from his instrument. She could hardly believe this was the man who would look down and barely nod when he shuffled past her in the hallway at the University. Sitting on the dais, he was whole and beautiful and perfect. His voice spiraled up into the black night sky and then descended to pierce Amira's heart.

After the initial awkward and shy conversations, the two people slowly opened their hearts. During stolen hours on their breaks at the University, they shared their dreams. They spoke of the plans to develop a four-year program leading to bachelor's degrees in arts and sciences. Nabil described the new campus that was slated to be built on the outskirts of the town of Birzeit and the Board of Trustees that would be formed to ensure the continuity of the school. Amira urged him to run for the board. Always shy in the presence of the opposite sex, Nabil forgot his inhibitions and basked in the glow of this remarkable woman's encouragement.

The prospect of marriage had never entered Nabil's mind, but he slowly came to realize that this special friendship could not continue without causing harm to Amira's reputation. She, in turn, lived for the snatches of time spent with him. Finally, Nabil hinted at approaching her father and was astounded when Amira agreed at once.

Carefully broaching the subject with her mother, Johara, Amira anticipated objections. She was surprised and pleased to find an immediate ally. "It is not fitting for a woman to be alone, and you will soon be too old to marry," her mother warned.

Enlisting the help of her three married daughters, Johara created a formidable cabal to confront her husband. Suliman argued and ranted and threatened. Then, as with Amira's education, he finally capitulated and agreed to receive "The Cripple" as he called him.

Nabil brought gifts of sweets and flowers for the house, American cigarettes for her father, and a gift box which he handed to her mother. He sat ramrod straight in the wicker chair across from Suliman and made all the correct thanksgivings and blessings before sipping his Turkish coffee. Amira watched the vein in his temple throb, the only sign of his racing heart. After an interminable amount of time, Suliman smiled and gave his blessing.

He found Nabil to be serious, polite and likable though he hated to admit it. His family was respectable and when seated, he was an attractive, if not handsome man. His daughter was well past her prime, and searching his conscience, Suliman could find no shame or dishonor in the pairing. Allah would be merciful, he thought as he motioned to his wife to give the small package wrapped in blue paper to Amira. She felt all eyes on her as she opened it, and then held up a thin beaten gold chain. Johara helped clasp it around her daughter's neck. Amira would never take it off.

Chapter Five

Decatur, GA

Karen cracked Sami's office door open and poked her head inside. "Knock, knock," she said. "Haven't you burned the midnight oil enough for one day?" Entering the office, she came around behind him. Dropping her hands to his shoulders, she began kneading the bunched up muscles.

"You are so tense," she admonished, "Relax." He obeyed willingly, closing his eyes and groaning softly. His body relaxed though his mind was still reeling.

"Did I hear your phone ring?" she asked, her hands doing wonderful things to the back of his neck.

"Mmm, telemarketer. Don't know how they get this number." He hated lying to her but couldn't think of a way to describe the call he just received, especially since he had no details yet.

"When are you coming to bed?" she asked, removing one hand to stifle a yawn.

"Soon," he replied, patting the hand that remained on his shoulder. "You go ahead, I won't be long." He looked up as she bent to kiss him. A curtain of hair fell across her cheek. She had changed into light cotton pajamas covered by a flowered robe. She smelled clean, like soap and shampoo.

"You work too hard," said Karen, her hand rubbing across the beginning of nighttime stubble on his cheek. "If you come before I fall asleep, I'll give you a back scratch."

"You're too good to me," he confessed.

"You're right," Karen agreed, and turned to pad

across the room, her terrycloth mules slapping gently on the floorboards. She paused in the doorway and turned to give him a smile and a mischievous wink. She left the door open.

Sami considered calling his parents' home in Ramallah, but it would be 3:00 am. He didn't want to alarm them. Turning over every possible scenario, as his rational mind told him to do, Sami could find no explanation. What could this mysterious Egyptian possibly want with him? Needing time to harness his emotions, he waited almost an hour before retiring. Karen knew him too well not to be suspicious.

He used the small half-bath, off his den, to wash before going upstairs. Creeping along the hallway, Sami winced at the creaking floorboards. Pausing at his daughter's room, he cracked open the door. The lavender walls were less garish in the glow of the nightlight. His daughter lay sleeping amidst a sea of pink and white ruffles. Her dark hair fanned across the pillow, her face turned away from him. Easing the door shut, he moved on down the hall to the master bedroom.

Karen was asleep, curled on her side like a child. In the dark, Sami shrugged out of his clothes and slipped into bed beside her. He listened to her even breathing, bracing himself for a hesitation, or a murmur. But she slept on in innocence. He was relieved. For now he would keep his foreboding to himself and wait for the promised messenger before deciding a course of action. He had no choice.

* * *

The summons came sooner than expected. Sami was seated in his study as the night before. Staring at the computer screen, he willed himself to concentrate on the unfinished report he was editing. The jangling phone startled him, even though he had been expecting it. The caller ID displayed 'Out of Area' and he snatched up the cordless receiver. Silence. But a palpable presence on the other end.

"Dr. Sami Nasser?" The voice was younger, less cultured than the Egyptian's. The accent was Palestinian or Jordanian.

"What do you want?" Sami demanded.

"To meet with you. We need to talk."

"Has this anything to do with my brother?"

Silence again.

"Answer me or I will hang up."

"He is well, *Inshallah*, and sends you his love. We must meet in person, Doctor. Shall I come to your home?"

Bile rose in Sami's throat. "There is a coffee shop called Java House on East Lake Drive. Do you know it?"

"I will find it. Shall we say tomorrow at noon?"

Sami scrolled through his calendar. "That is not a good time," he replied. "I can be there at two o'clock. How will I know you?"

"I will find you," came the response. "*Ma'a as-salaamah.*"

Come to his home?

Sami fought to keep his temper. He vowed that whatever game these people were playing would end tomorrow. He had finally contacted his parent's home in Ramallah that morning. His mother was delighted to hear from him and asked many questions about her granddaughter. His father sounded distant and old.

Guilt stabbed at Sami's heart, as it always did when he spoke with his father. As the eldest son, he knew it was his duty to be with his parents, and he was not. He knew they were proud of him, but it was not enough to compensate for the loss.

Kamal lived in the family home now and was a good son. He had married two years ago when Sami and Karen were visiting, and his wife had recently borne her first child, a boy. The two brothers had discussed Sami's vocation several times, and Kamal assured him it was not wrong to follow his calling. Each man has a destiny and must decide which path to take.

When Sami asked to speak with Kamal, there was
a pause. "He has been away from home for a time," replied
Amira. "You know he is on the board with the university now
and is required to travel. Do you wish to speak to his wife?" she
continued. "She knows more than I."

"No," replied Sami. If Kamal's wife did indeed know
anything, she would not speak of it over the phone. "Give
everyone my love and I will call again soon. *Ma'a as-salaamah
emmi.*"

Chapter Six

Ramallah, West Bank of Israel
1975

After two years of marriage, Sami's birth came as a surprise and a blessing to Nabil and Amira. The little boy had his father's beauty, his mother's wit, and the intelligence of both parents. Sami was named after his paternal grandfather, as was the custom. The name translated to sublime, and he was doted on by the entire extended family. Three years later, when another son was born, the couple gave thanks to Allah's beneficence for the double blessing, and the boy was named Kamal for perfection.

Nabil and Amira were practicing Muslims who raised their boys to be inquisitive. Nabil demanded a "striving for perfection" in all tasks which he considered to be the ultimate tribute to Allah. He saw no dichotomy between religion and science. Indeed, he viewed all superstition as offensive and liked to point out that it was Muslims who pioneered mathematics and science when the West wallowed in ignorance.

Sami loved and admired his father, but at times, chafed under his strict rule. When Nabil vetoed his son's appointment to a soccer team, Amira deferred to Nabil's judgment, but the spark in her eyes caused her husband to reconsider his decision. Nabil had little respect for games or physical pursuits, perhaps because he had been barred from them all his life. Sami was sternly warned that his studies could not suffer. And they did not. As elder brothers do, he eased the path for Kamal.

As long as the boys did well in school, Nabil grudgingly allowed them to attend the local cinema as a treat. Below the flickering screen, the brothers slouched, side by side, in the smoke-filled theater. Munching on sunflower seeds, they spit the shells on the floor.

Films fell into three groups, each possessing its own charm. The first consisted of Indian films from Bollywood. Kamal enjoyed the exaggerated antics of the heroes. He cheered and hooted, with the rest of the audience, during the contrived fight scenes and car chases. Music dominated the movies, interspersed with simple dialogue translated into subtitles in Arabic and Hebrew—often with hilarious results. Less interested in the plot, both boys enjoyed ogling the dusky and voluptuous heroines as they warbled in high pitched voices and danced in bejeweled saris that swirled across the screen.

The old black and white movies, filmed in Egypt during the forties and fifties, made up the second group. Sami was mesmerized by the music icons that influenced his father. Farid Al Atrash had died the year before Sami was born, but audiences still thrilled to his unique voice, high and mellow in his youth, deep and rich as he aged. The boys never tired of hearing Farid's *mawals*, the slow improvisations of a few poetic lines that often lasted up to 15 minutes. It reminded Sami of Nabil, who was known for his *mawals* when he played at local weddings.

The storylines in these films were melodramatic and inevitably about unrequited love. Sami's favorite actor was the handsome and charismatic Abdul Halim Hafez, whom his father regarded as the greatest male musician in the Arab world. Sami hugged himself as he sat in the dark, enthralled by the young singer who exuded such passion with his powerful voice it earned him the titles of Nightingale and King of Romance.

Sami pictured his father as a young man and considered him as handsome and talented as the actors on the screen. When Sami voiced this opinion during an evening meal, Nabil responded gruffly.

"The cinema fills your head with foolishness!" he had grumbled. But Amira smiled.

The music touched Sami's soul, but it was the beautiful Egyptian actress, Faten Hamama, who stole his heart the first time he saw her in *Angel of Mercy*. She was fifteen when the movie was made and became the epitome of female perfection that Sami carried in his heart. Well past childhood, the image would remain.

The third group included American movies. The westerns were, by far, the most popular among young boys. The actors seldom sang, but they rode horses, drove cattle, and shot villains. Like the Bedouin, they were warriors with a code of honor. The landscapes were vast with wide skies and soaring mountains.

Sami and Kamal vowed to go to America one day where they would live on a ranch and become cowboys.

* * *

The Israeli Civil Administration (CA) was established in 1981 and put in charge of tax collection and land expropriation. This included olive groves that Arab villagers had tended for generations. Jewish settlements sprouted up and prevented the expansion of Ramallah and virtually cut it off from the surrounding villages. Over the next six years, as resentment and unrest grew in the town, residents were jailed or deported to neighboring countries for their membership in the Palestinian Liberation Organization.

In 1987, when the First Intifada broke out, Sami was twelve. Many Ramallah residents were among the early joiners. Bulletins were distributed weekly on the streets with a schedule of the daily protests, strikes, and actions against Israeli patrols in the city.

Walking home from school one afternoon, Sami and

Kamal found themselves caught up in a demonstration. The street ahead roiled with a sea of surging bodies. Black smoke seethed from a pile of burning tires, and the boys covered their noses and mouths to keep from choking. Sami put a protective arm around his nine-year-old brother who clung to him.

Searching the streets for an escape, Sami spotted the father of a schoolmate. He watched as the man lit a rag stuffed into a bottle of liquid and then tossed it at a group of Israeli soldiers. The Molotov cocktail was deflected by a riot shield and exploded in the crowd. Men and boys scrambled to avoid the fire; the unlucky ones screaming and flapping their arms to douse the flames. The Israelis, outfitted in their formidable gear, responded with a volley of rubber bullets and tear gas. The world had gone mad.

Through the smoke, Sami spotted a narrow alley the brothers had sometimes used as a shortcut. Grabbing Kamal by the collar, he half-dragged him to safety. They both collapsed against the rough stone walls of the house on the corner.

"I dropped my school books," said Kamal, tears rolling down his smooth brown cheeks.

"Me too," said Sami. "Don't worry, I'll get us home."

Kamal nodded, "I know."

* * *

Birzeit University was closed seven times for a total of 11 months between years 84-87. House arrests in Ramallah resumed and curfews were imposed restricting travel and exports. Local schools were shut down. In response, Nabil and Amira organized home schooling sessions to help students make up missed material. The dining room was transformed into a makeshift schoolroom where Sami and Kamal, along with neighbor boys, bent heads to their studies. Amira taught a group of girls in the adjoining front room, a curtain strung across the doorway for modesty.

This was the first time Sami fully appreciated Nabil's brilliance in mathematics. When windows were shuttered to block out the erupting streets below, the boy hardly noticed the tumult or the stifling air from lack of ventilation. He reveled in an inner world created by the beauty and logic of his father's words.

The home school was Nabil's symbol of civil disobedience. He eschewed violence, and his greatest fear was that his sons might fall victim to the PLO recruiting tactics. They were still boys, but he knew that is when fanatics target the mind and soul.

Nabil would point to the refugee camps only miles away or to Nablus where armed militias roamed the streets. "Is this how we should live?" he demanded. Sami agreed with his father. He hoped to become a doctor and a healer. Violence and wanton destruction held no attraction for him. The action he enjoyed in the cinema was far removed from the mayhem that took place before his eyes.

Kamal was more restive. He chaffed at being restricted to the house and missed his playmates. He would peek through the wooden shutters when no one was looking, and observe the chaos below. One evening, as an Israeli patrol passed, Kamal saw a group of three boys, not much older than himself, dart from an alley and throw rocks. Several soldiers raised their guns threateningly, but did nothing. The boys melted back into the alley as quickly as they had emerged. Kamal smiled.

Chapter Seven

Decatur, GA

Through streaked window panes, Sami watched dark clouds blossoming like bruises in the gray sky. He had hoped for a seat in the back, but a window table was all that was available. His eyes scanned the room as he inhaled the scent of freshly brewed coffee. Weathered brick covered the bottom portion of the walls. Mottled plaster adorned the top half with artsy black and white photos scattered across the expanse. Sami had been there only once before when he shared lunch with a coworker. It was the first restaurant that came to mind when he was asked to name a meeting place.

Sami's hands clasped a stout coffee mug, the contents barely touched. The room bustled with young people of all sizes and shapes. At the table next to him, a pimply-faced boy was pecking away at his laptop and nibbling on a wedge of pita bread smeared with hummus. The skinny girl across from him was sipping a latte as she stared at the screen of her Mac, its light reflecting on her pale face. Sami wondered if people talked anymore.

A female employee looked up as a young man entered the coffee shop. He was dressed in jeans and a loose dark shirt and looked like a foreign grad student. She watched him hesitate as he scanned the room. "Can I help you?" she asked from behind the counter.

"Excuse me?" he replied, taking a step back.

"Can I help you?" she repeated with less animation as his eyes bored into her.

"I am meeting someone," he answered sweeping the room again until his eyes came to rest on Sami. "Never mind, I see my companion," he added, with a dismissive gesture.

"Yes sir," she smiled sweetly. Turning to her fellow employee who was busy making a fresh pot of mocha java, she grimaced and mouthed, "Fucking foreigners!"

Sami was startled by the young man who materialized beside his table.

"May I join you, Doctor?" the man inquired. His smile was polite, but it did not reach his eyes. Sami nodded but said nothing. He estimated the man to be late twenties. Of average height and lean, he was neither handsome nor unattractive. He would easily blend into the campus. His most arresting feature was a set of arched black brows that nearly met in the middle of his high forehead. They framed intelligent dark eyes that burned with a fanatic's intensity.

"*As-salaamu aleikum. Ismi Khalid bin Ali.*"

"What is your business with me Khalid bin Ali?" Sami inquired, meeting the penetrating gaze with equal scrutiny.

"Business?" the young man echoed, switching to English. "I bring greetings from your family and your homeland."

Sami let the words hang between them before replying. "Communication with my family is private. No intermediary is needed. I am a busy man. If this is a shake-down for some non-existent charity, I have no interest."

Khalid feigned a look of confusion and opened his hands palms up on the table. "I assure you I am only a messenger. I ask for nothing."

A young waitress paused by their table. Her streaky blonde hair was pulled back in a loose knot, and she drew out a pencil that had been perched on her ear. "Would you like to order now?" she inquired, glancing at Khalid and then back at Sami.

"I'll have another coffee," Sami answered, and looked

inquiringly at his companion across the table.

"Hot tea please," Khalid responded.

"Would you like any particular type?" the girl asked, her pale eyes registering fatigue and boredom.

"No," Khalid threw an annoyed glance at the offending female whose whorish attire and easy familiarity deeply offended him. "Just black tea."

"Yes sir," the waitress replied. Sami watched her pale eyes flicker to life for an instant and then turn bland as she scribbled the order.

"Thank you," said Sami as she turned to leave.

"So what is your message?" he inquired, turning back to Khalid.

"I do not have specific instructions yet, but I am told you are a very influential man who has knowledge we may need. We must call on all our brothers to help us succeed in our holy war."

The boy at the adjoining table glanced in their direction and then returned to his laptop. Lowering his voice, Sami switched to Arabic. "I am not your brother, and I have no interest in your holy war or your perversion of Islam."

Khalid gave a tight smile. "I see you believe the propaganda. You believe the West has accepted you, but that is a delusion. They will turn on you and your family just as they turned on the Japanese during World War II."

He paused as the waitress returned with his tea and refreshed Sami's coffee. Frowning, he kept his eyes on the table and waited for her to leave before continuing.

"You see, I am a student of history, and I understand my enemy well."

Sami shook his head. "Then you should know this is a war you cannot win."

"Oh, we can win Doctor, and we will. Plans are already being drawn for the mosque that will rise on the site of our greatest victory in New York. When the infidels kill our leaders, we replace them. The West cannot prevent our attacks because they are random and unpredictable. They cannot outmaneuver us because we constantly change our tactics and use their own technologies against them. In the end, we will destroy the networks that support their economies, and the West will go down."

"I've heard your message," said Sami, fishing in his pocket for his wallet. "We have nothing more to discuss, Khalid bin Ali."

He stood, pulled out two bills and tossed them on the table. "Stay away from my family," he warned, "or you will regret it. As you said, I am a man of influence."

Khalid stood as well, looking up at his adversary and hating him for it. "It will be your decision," he responded, "to stand with your brothers in victory or go down in defeat with the unbelievers."

* * *

Khalid watched the tall man weave between the tables as he exited the restaurant. Then he glanced at the two ten-dollar bills that had been thrown down so casually. His lips curved downward.

Turning his head, he saw the yellow-haired whore watching, waiting for him to leave, so she could collect her money. He turned abruptly and followed the doctor. The rain had stopped and the sky was clearing. A timid sun poked out between the clouds and steam rose from puddles in the street.

Khalid slipped dark glasses out of his pocket and put them on. He looked both ways down the street bustling with pedestrians, but Sami had disappeared. A girl whizzed by him on a bike, and he stepped back on the curb. Her jean cutoffs clung to well-muscled thighs, and a fitted white halter set off her gleaming bronze skin. The sun bounced off her iridescent blue helmet. Khalid blinked, and registered his surroundings to determine if anyone was watching him. Crossing the street and heading towards his car, he turned his thoughts inward. He had not expected the doctor to be this illogical or difficult. It was not a good omen.

Chapter Eight

"Sami, did you hear what I said?" Karen asked. She reached across the kitchen table and rustled the newspaper until Sami's eyes appeared, inquisitive and owlish, above the pages. "I told my parents that Mira and I would come to Haig Point on Wednesday and stay for a few days. Are you sure there is no way you can join us? It would make Dad so happy."

Sami folded the paper with a sigh. "My conference is Monday night, and I fly back Tuesday. I am just not sure I can get the time off. You know everything is in upheaval with the new director."

He read the disappointment in her eyes, but she said nothing. Taking a sip of her coffee, she wrinkled her nose as she discovered the brew was cold. Even in a frumpy bathrobe with her hair twisted up in a knot, she managed to look beautiful.

"Okay," he relented. "I'll see if I can make it later in the week. It would be nice to get in a game of golf." Sami thought about his father-in-law. John Cameron had been his mentor and the head of neurology at Emory. It might be a good idea to confide in him and get his advice. John knew how to be discreet.

Karen came around the table and gave her husband a quick hug. He squeezed her back, but countered, "No promises Karen. I'll do the best I can, okay?"

"Okey dokey," she replied, retrieving the coffee pot to refresh their cups. She carried her mug to the back stairs and called up to her daughter. "Mira, you need to come down now, or you'll be late for school." Karen was still getting used to her daughter's independence. They picked out clothes the night before, but Mira now insisted on dressing and grooming herself. Karen heard a thump, thump, thump, as the little girl came down the stairs and dragged a bulging vinyl backpack behind her.

"What's that, honey bun?" she asked adjusting a headband to push back the dark curls from her daughter's face.

"I'm taking some of my horses for show and tell."

Sami set down his paper again. "They allow horses in your school?" he asked in mock amazement.

"Oh Daddy! You know they aren't real." Mira ran to his arms for a morning hug and kiss. "Do you want to see which ones I'm taking?"

"I think you had better eat your breakfast first before Mommy starts yelling at us."

"I don't yell," Karen quipped as she set a glass of juice and a bowl of cereal topped with blueberries in front of her daughter. "Somebody needs to keep you two moving."

"Mmmm, booberries," said Mira as she carefully poured milk into her bowl. They were her favorite fruit since before she could say the word, and her mispronunciation stuck. She munched happily while perusing the back of the cereal box, as Karen prepared her lunch, and Sami checked his briefcase.

It was the usual morning routine of a perfectly ordinary day. Karen kissed her husband and daughter goodbye. Sami paused at the door. "If you're near Emory today, why don't we meet for lunch."

She raised her eyebrows. "That would be nice, what time?"

"Noonish." He winked and flashed a smile that would make her agree to anything.

"Daddy, come on!" Mira urged, juggling her backpack and lunchbox.

"The princess calls," said Sami, turning to leave. Karen

watched them settle into his sleek black BMW and waved as they exited the garage and headed out into the world.

Back in her kitchen, Karen hummed as she cleared the table and loaded the dishwasher. The mindless chores gave her time to organize the day in her head. A note to Mira's teacher excusing her from school, a trip to the post office, a one hour jog followed by a quick shower, and then lunch with Sami. That would leave the entire afternoon free to work on her writing, update her blog, and tweak her website.

"Hallelujah, Hallelujah…" the song from Shrek kept looping through her head. "Good grief," Karen moaned, "I really need to get away."

Chapter Nine

Atlanta, GA

Khalid glanced at his watch and shifted the cardboard sign tucked under his arm. The South Terminal of Hartsfield Jackson International Airport reminded him of a huge anthill with people scurrying back and forth dragging their burdens. He stood in the midst of a crowd just past the baggage claim. They all waited for some person or some group. Many appeared to be foreigners, like him.

A new wave of passengers spilled from the escalator, so he pulled out his sign and held it aloft. The sign read, "Emory Students." The flight from London, carrying the two-man team assigned to him, had landed forty minutes ago. He knew they would have to pass through customs which could take time. It should all go smoothly though. The Americans' fear of racial profiling would ensure his men received little scrutiny.

Just two weeks earlier he had entered this same airport. He observed the custom agents as he'd been taught and remained amiable and polite. The overweight employee stamped his passport and handed it back with a smile. How easy it is, Khalid marveled, to enter the United States.

The man who met him was a sleeper who had lived in Atlanta for ten years and worked as a cab driver. The name on his cab identification card read: Abdul Al-Awan. His skin was swarthy and pockmarked. He had let his hair grow to comb across his balding pate. Khalid guessed he was Syrian, but neither man offered to exchange personal information.

The driver took Khalid to a car rental agency where

he rented a black Ford sedan. Afterwards, Khalid followed Al-Awan to an efficiency apartment just off Buford Highway. Khalid thanked the man who handed him a set of keys and a business card containing information about the next contact. He pocketed the keys and watched as Al-Awan drove off. Despite his reticence, the cab driver knew what Khalid looked like, where he resided, and what type of car he was driving. That could be dangerous.

Glancing down at the small white card, Khalid saw it advertised a pawn shop most likely in the neighborhood. He would find the place and go that night to obtain the weapons. He felt naked in this strange place without a gun. He knew from research that at one time, Atlanta was known as the murder capital of the United States.

Khalid was jerked back to the present by a man next to him who bent down to retrieve the placard he had dropped at Khalid's feet. "Excuse me," the man apologized.

"No matter," replied Khalid, his eyes scrutinizing the large black man who now loomed above him. The man wore a dark suit and sported a military looking cap. He was sweating profusely and his teeth shone brilliant white against his ebony skin.

Khalid spun around when he heard a woman shriek, "There, that must be our limo driver! Come on y'all!"

The black man was soon surrounded by a gaggle of cackling middle-aged women. Khalid stared at their garish clothing and chunky jewelry. They giggled and flirted with the big black man as if they were still girls. A tall gangly woman, with shoulder-length bleached hair, looked over at Khalid and smiled. He turned away, fighting to keep the disgust from his face.

He moved closer to the escalator where the emerging procession had dwindled to a trickle. Khalid knew very little about the men he was meeting except their names and the assurance they had trained in the Yemeni camps and were prepared to carry out their duty. Visitor visas had been produced like magic, along with international driver licenses. It was a first visit to the States for both men, and neither had any traceable record.

A tall man paused about twenty feet away and nudged his smaller companion, pointing to Khalid's sign. The smaller man nodded and they started towards him. Both looked like Middle Easterners but were dressed in the American uniform of jeans, t-shirts and sneakers. The shorter man was about Khalid's height though slighter in build. His expression remained serious while the big man smiled, revealing a set of perfect teeth. Khalid disliked him instantly.

"You are Khalid," the big man said in English with only the trace of an accent.

"Yes, welcome to Atlanta. I trust you did not check luggage?" They both affirmed and gestured to their duffle bags.

"Good. We will proceed to the car," said Khalid, turning away. The men exchanged glances and followed their leader through baggage claim where giant conveyer belts transported the suitcases and bags that spewed from central holding compartments. Khalid paused at the door to crumple his sign and toss it into a trash can before exiting into the sunshine of a humid afternoon.

Chapter Ten

London, England

The Teacher thanked the waiter who set a steaming cup of mint tea in front of him. The young man's uniform was impeccable. A shock of neatly combed auburn hair set off his ruddy English complexion. The Teacher lifted his porcelain cup carefully by the handle and sniffed the aromatic mint.

"It is good to enjoy the comforts of home in a foreign land," he said to the middle-aged Saudi seated across from him.

"Yes," his guest replied, "Just so." The two men were dressed in business attire and seated in the Palm Court of the Ritz Hotel where a formal tea was served each afternoon at 3:30.

The Teacher smiled. "The staff here is most...obliging." He eyed the delicate cucumber and smoked salmon sandwiches, fresh cream scones, and tasteful selection of pastries displayed on silver cake stands.

"What do you think of the renovation?" he continued. The extensive project to renovate the hotel began after 1995 when the hotel was returned to private British ownership. It was not completed until ten years later.

Gazing around the room, the Saudi appraised the marble columns, gilt moldings, crystal chandeliers, and of course, the palms which added a touch of home. "How very obliging," he thought, parroting The Teacher's observation.

The extravagant Louis XVI décor complemented the magnificent French chateau exterior. He recalled staring up at the huge copper lions on the corners of the roof the first time he had visited the hotel with his father. He now considered it the only place to stay in London, other than the Savoy which was currently under renovation.

His wives and daughters preferred Paris, of course, where they could purchase the latest in French fashion. But he liked the English loyalty to their monarchy, and their respect for ceremony and custom.

"Exquisite," he replied, "I understand it cost over £50 million.

"Everything has its price," said The Teacher.

"Indeed it does," replied the Saudi, rubbing a brown finger alongside his temple.

The Teacher surveyed the room to ensure the tables around them were unoccupied. The two men sat in a small alcove recessed from the main room. "Are you certain of your information on the shipment?" he asked, a genial smile frozen on his face.

"This opportunity is a gift from heaven," the Saudi responded. "A significant blunder on the part of our enemy. My source is very well placed and has ties to my family. If anything had changed, he would notify me."

Nodding, the Teacher took a sip of his tea. "Our team is in place now. They have been instructed to obtain a shipment date from the source. They know nothing more."

The Saudi inspected the pastry tray finally selecting one with silver tongs and setting it on his plate. "I am curious about your source," he said. "How did you find him?"

The Teacher hesitated before replying. "The English have a saying, *curiosity killed the cat.*" However, I am pleased to oblige you." He glanced around the room again, before selecting a cucumber sandwich for himself and offering to refill their tea cups.

"A young man in Ramallah came to my attention through our Palestinian contacts. He has apparently flirted with our cause for some time, though he made no overtures.

His family is educated and they are good Muslims. He may be of future use, but his brother is already in place in America. He is a doctor in a prominent position with connections to the organization of interest. He should be able to obtain the information we need."

"That is good," said the Saudi, taking a bite of his pastry and relishing the tart cherry filling. He knew the Egyptians to be clever and wily and could not resist needling the self-important man seated across from him. "Are you certain this doctor will cooperate?" he inquired, brushing several crumbs off the sleeve of his expensive suit. "Sometimes these so-called American Arabs become soft and corrupted by the comforts of the West."

"Ah, an interesting question. We must all be on guard against this danger," replied The Teacher. "As you know, I have a team in place. They have received training in Yemen, and their loyalty is beyond question."

The Saudi raised his wiry salt and pepper brows and nodded approval.

Setting down the cup of tea and steepling his long fingers, The Teacher continued. "If the doctor has strayed from the true path, I am sure he can be persuaded to return to the fold. My team leader is intelligent and ambitious; he understands the price of failure. And all of them have reason to hate our common enemy."

"As do we all," confirmed the Saudi.

"We understand each other," said The Teacher, his eyes sparking to life. "When next we meet, my brother, there will be cause for celebration. *Inshallah.*"

"*Inshallah,*" the Saudi echoed.

"How long will you stay in London?" asked The Teacher.

"I leave for Jeddah tomorrow." Gazing around the lush room, the Saudi caught his reflection in the ornate beveled mirrors lining the wall. He sighed. In twenty four hours he would exchange his hand tailored linen suit for a white cotton *thobe* and don a red checkered *kefiyyeh*."

Chapter Eleven

Chamblee, GA

Khalid stared at the display on his phone before thumbing the answer button. After a brief pause, the voice of The Teacher reverberated clear and strong across the line.

"Is this Khalid?" He spoke in Arabic with a distinct Egyptian accent. Khalid had never met the man, but he recognized his voice and knew his reputation.

"Yes, it is good to hear from you," he replied. They exchanged the required greetings and blessings while Khalid's mind raced.

"Is all well with your brothers?" asked The Teacher, meaning: *"Have you met with the other operatives and is all well?"*

"Yes all is well with us, thanks be to God," Khalid replied.

"Will you be coming to visit us soon?" The Teacher continued. *"Have you accomplished your mission?"*

"*Inshallah*," said Khalid, "As soon as I can determine a date." *"I don't have the information yet."*

There was long pause.

"We have been very busy." Khalid added and bit his lip.

"I understand," the silken voice continued, "But your family misses you. When will you have a travel date?"

"Soon, soon, *Inshallah*" Khalid smiled, hoping his voice sounded reassuring.

"Do not disappoint us," said The Teacher. *"Ma'a as-salaamah."*

Khalid punched the end button on his phone and

marveled at the technology that carried a human voice halfway around the world. But then, The Teacher could be anywhere. Khalid had never trusted Egyptians with their smooth oily voices and thinly disguised distain for the rest of the Arab world.

"Well, I am no gullible villager," he thought. "If I succeed in this mission, I will gain the respect I deserve. Then I will be giving the orders."

Chapter Twelve

London, England

The Teacher slipped the disposable cell phone into his pocket and decided he should replace it soon. He was careful to keep his conversations neutral, but better to error on the side of caution. The Americans were weak but not stupid.

He cursed the Saudi for planting this seed of doubt in his mind. Did the House of Saud truly believe that throwing money at The Cause would save them? While those hypocrites appeased the Americans and plotted with the Jews, The Teacher planned and orchestrated the battles that would bring final victory. What right did that fat sycophant have to question him?

Cracking the window curtain of his room at the Dorchester Hotel, he looked down at the snarl of traffic crawling along Park Lane in the late afternoon drizzle. He'd always considered England to be a dreary place, since his days at Oxford University. The small country had an impressive history, but it was a nation past its prime. The sun had long since set on the British Empire. They would be doomed with the rest of Europe.

Still fuming, he crossed the room to the wet bar and surveyed the miniature bottles. Scotch? *Too medicinal.* Vodka? *Too Russian.* Wine? *Why bother.* He settled on a bottle of Remy Martin cognac. Swirling the amber liquid in an oversized snifter, he inhaled the delightful perfume.

He was unused to alcohol, and the fiery liquid had an immediate soothing effect. The prophet was wise to forbid such a potent drug. It made men foolish. He dropped into an easy chair opposite the bed and surveyed the room. It was modest in comparison with the lavish suite his Saudi compatriot enjoyed at the Ritz. But the decor was tasteful and traditional, and The Teacher did not require luxury.

Cream-colored paneling produced a pleasing backdrop for the richly patterned damask drapes. He switched on a bedside lamp which illuminated hues of gold and burgundy and created a microcosm of warmth against the gloom and damp beyond the windows. He studied a vintage collection of hunting scenes arranged on the wall above a small antique desk.

Tally-ho!

The Teacher took a sip of his drink. His father had been an Anglophile like so many Egyptians from his generation. Hence the Teacher's undergraduate degree from Oxford. But he had never shared his father's admiration for the British. He found the majority of them to be stuffy and unimaginative. If he felt any affinity with the West, it would be for the Germans.

The Nazis had made a valiant effort to rule but had lost. At present, the Germans supplied the nations of Islam with the technology for war. But sadly it was only out of greed. In the end it would not save them. The Teacher revered the philosophy of Friedrich Nietzsche above all others. His theory of "the will to power" provided the basis for understanding motivation in human behavior. What people really want is power. The heroes and masters of history did not desire mere living but wanted power, glory, and greatness. The Germans had understood this at one time, but unfortunately their progeny were indolent and self-serving.

The Russians were another matter. They had always been corrupt but never weak. They were godless, however, and thus bereft of hope. A spiritual vacuum will always be filled, in Russia's case, with vodka, drugs, and artificial nationalism. Russia had slunk out of Afghanistan in defeat. Muslim nations had her surrounded and bit at her heels like jackals. It was just a matter of time before the bear would be pulled down.

The Americans presented an interesting dichotomy. Many still practiced their religion, and the churches were not empty sepulchers like the cathedrals of Europe. But the believers were relentlessly bombarded by a hostile media, and the culture was degenerating quickly with the advent of the internet. Self-indulgent citizens elected leaders who were weak and debauched. Unchecked consumption and greed generated a national debt that was spiraling out of control.

The Teacher picked up the remote and clicked on the news. He preferred to watch the English or European channels. *Know thine enemy.* A voluptuous blond with a painted face rattled off details of the American President's most recent vacation. The Teacher smiled, recalling the shock in the Arab world when this same man bowed to the king of Saudi Arabia and apologized for his country. After the last world war, America was feared. No longer. She was ripe for a fall, and now was the time for action.

He clicked through several more channels while he finished his drink, then shut off the television. He remained seated, staring at the black screen. He tried to remember the last time he had visited the United States.

Chapter Thirteen

Decatur, GA

It was 11:45 when Sami glanced up at the clock. Unconsciously tapping his pen on the desk, he was reviewing a case record from his morning rounds when his secretary, Dolores, knocked and cracked open the door.

"I'm sorry," she said with worry lines etched across her forehead. "There is a young man here who insists he has an appointment with you. I am afraid he refuses to leave."

Sami slammed shut the folder in front of him and rose from his chair. "Show him in."

It had been several days since they met, but Sami remembered Khalid bin Ali well. They remained silent at first as they sized each other up.

"How dare you come to my office!" Sami's voice was low with barely controlled fury. "You are making a very big mistake."

"You are the one who is mistaken, Doctor. You have ignored my calls. That is foolish. We can reach you anywhere, at your office or at your home. You must know that."

"Get out before I call security!" Sami took a step forward.

Khalid put up his hands. "I am only here to deliver a message. We require your assistance. There will be a transport from the CDC to Dugway Proving Ground in the near future. We need the date and time."

"What delivery? I don't know what you're talking about."

"*What* doesn't concern you. *When* is what we need to

know."

"I don't have access to that information, and I wouldn't tell you if I did. You must be mad."

Khalid's dark eyes flickered, but his face remained impassive. "You can get access Doctor. It would be in your best interest to do so."

"Is that a threat?" Sami asked, trying to read the man's eyes.

"We don't make threats. We carry out the will of Allah." His composure breaking, Khalid gestured with his hands to encompass the office. "You think all of this makes you superior to us. You live in your big house and drive your expensive car while your brothers live in squalor under the Jews. We ask one favor that is your duty to provide. You are a Muslim!"

Sami shook his head as if to clear his mind. "You don't speak for my God. You delivered your message and you have my answer. Now get out!"

Khalid nodded, "I will report your answer," and he turned to go. Stopping at the door, he looked back at the photograph on a shelf in back of Sami's desk.

"That is your wife and daughter, is it not?" he asked. "May Allah protect them."

Sami felt the blood drain from his face and his hands trembled. "If you touch my family I will kill you."

"I told you, we do not make threats," Khalid protested. "I am asking for cooperation. You should reconsider."

Just then Sami heard Karen greeting Dolores in the outer office. Before Sami could react, Khalid opened the door and found himself face to face with Karen. She was far more beautiful than her photo.

"Oh," she exclaimed. "I'm sorry. I didn't know anyone was here." She shot a look at Sami and then looked back to the young man in the doorway.

He stared at her, his eyes so penetrating she felt as

though she were a bug under a microscope. "I was just leaving," he said with a dismissive nod.

"We will meet again Doctor," he said to Sami, and then he was gone.

Karen shivered and involuntarily hugged herself. "My God who was that?" she asked, noting her husband's unusually pale face.

He shrugged and forced a smile. "A new exchange student at Emory. He is actually a nephew of Moussa Hayek. Do you remember him?"

"Yes, of course. His wife Nawal and I worked on a committee together last year. He is their nephew? He seemed so…" she struggled for the word, "crude".

"Well he is new here and it will take him time to adjust. But I know what you mean. He is an intense young man."

"Disturbing would be a better word," she responded. "He actually looked through me." She shivered again. "I hope you won't have to deal with him. He looks like trouble."

Sami was impressed by his wife's perception and realized he would have to be very careful. He did not want her dragged into this. But he decided he had to do something. For the first time, he believed this man might be serious.

"As we say in the Middle East, *kus emmo*," he said taking her arm. "What is your pleasure for lunch, my love."

Karen laughed. "I'm so glad you taught me all the best curse words. That is so appropriate."

Chapter Fourteen

Amman, Jordan
1999

Laila ya Laila, ya bint Abu Laila...
The song swam in Khalid's head. Sitting in the driver's seat of his car, he squeezed his eyes shut and massaged his temples.

Laila, the daughter of his father's younger brother, Abu Laila. The unfortunate man had only girls, so his title was derived from the name of his eldest daughter.

Laila ya sumara...
Laila the dark, with black hair but eyes the color of the sea at dusk. Dormant crusader blood? Perhaps that is what cursed her. Like the doctor's wife who had looked at him so boldly, Laila's eyes were her weapon.

His father and uncle built neighboring houses in Amman. Khalid was the eldest of five boys and three girls. He dedicated his time to his studies and the Koran and was considered a talented scholar. He was handsome and well formed but average in height which he made up for with intensity. His younger brothers, though taller, never questioned his commands.

Being the eldest, Khalid basked in the attention showered on him by his father and uncle. He worked hard to remain at the top of his class and burned with a desire to excel. Laila, he knew from his uncle's comments, was also intelligent and consistently won honors at her school. This irritated him, but he was not sure why. She was a girl, what did it matter?

As a skinny child, Laila had never drawn his attention.

But then she blossomed. One night during the Ramadan feast at his uncle's house, Khalid's eyes followed her as she poured tea and passed platters of sweets. She was still slender but now graceful, her movements fluid. She kept her eyes down as she served. When she reached him, Khalid selected a piece of cake and a glass of mint tea.

"*Shukran,*" he said.

"*Afwan,*" she replied, looking him full in the face for just a second. Her eyes gleamed like jewels, not green or blue but some color in between. She quickly moved on and then withdrew carrying her empty platter. She did not reappear the rest of the night.

Near dawn, and still unable to sleep, Khalid climbed up to the flat rooftop of his father's house. He breathed in the balmy air perfumed by the scent of lemon trees and jasmine. He looked up at the fading stars and then gazed across the city, a warren of brick and stone dotted with soaring minarets. He was startled by the sound of a soft voice and instinctively ducked behind a scraggly potted palm. Then he saw her.

Laila was walking along the rooftop on the building across from him, a book perched in her hands. She was reciting from it, but Khalid couldn't make out the words. Her head was uncovered, and he could see her dark hair drawn back simply to form a long thick braid. Back and forth she walked, never taking her eyes from the book. Her lips moved continuously and the lilt of her voice drifted to him on the wind.

As the sun broke the horizon, she closed her book. She looked west towards his house and paused, resting her arms on the wall atop her roof. He could just make out her face. When she looked towards the palm that was hiding him, he held his breath. She turned abruptly and descended the stone staircase while he watched the lightening sky washed deep blue tinged with green, the color of Laila's eyes.

For the next two weeks, Khalid returned each night to

watch her, only retreating when she left the rooftop. He lay in his bed in the hours before dawn and stared at the white-washed ceiling, unable to sleep. His mind and body burned with a yearning that was foreign to him until now. He prayed but to no avail. The remaining days of Ramadan passed in a blur, his mind sluggish from the combined lack of sleep and nutrition. For the first time, his studies suffered, and his teachers were displeased.

He relished the fasting and thirst, welcoming their cleansing effect. He vowed to purify his thoughts and think only of his duties to Allah and his family. But after breaking the fast at sunset, the corruption of his body overcame the noble intentions of his soul. He would creep up to the rooftop in the early hours before dawn in an agony of anticipation. What if she was not there?

In his mind, Khalid replayed the conversations he would have with her. But that could never happen unless they became engaged. Marriage between the children of brothers was blessed and condoned. He had no doubt his father and uncle would be overjoyed. But he planned to leave soon to study abroad at the University of Berlin. The burden of a wife and family was not appealing.

If there were only some way to gage her feelings for him. She had looked him full in the face, brief though it had been. And she came every night on the rooftop to be seen. Was it a message to him? He composed his note at least twenty times.

~~From the night your eyes first wounded me...~~
~~Have pity on my torment...~~

He settled on two sentences.

Fairest of the fair, bathed in the moon's bright glow. Give me some spark of hope that you might return my love, and I will be yours.

Under a pretext of delivering tomatoes from his mother's garden, Khalid went to his uncle's house. He spoke politely with his aunt in the kitchen for a while before exiting to the courtyard.

The staircase to the roof was on his left. Checking that he was alone, he quickly ascended the stone steps. He scanned the barren space and pictured his beloved stepping across the same tiles where he now stood. A large clay pot stood empty in the corner. Its contents had long since withered under the brutal sun. He thought this a good place to leave his note. He propped it carefully beside the pot, not too conspicuous but noticeable. He looked across at his own house and anticipated the coming night.

* * *

The stars shone bright against a black sky. Khalid had come earlier to the rooftop than usual. On the way, he woke one of his younger brothers and had to admonish the boy to go back to sleep. This was dangerous, and he knew it could not continue. He hoped for a resolution tonight.

When she finally appeared, he let out a sigh of relief. It was the last night of Ramadan, and he feared she would not come. She made her usual trek, pausing now and then to look up at the sky. When she reached the Northeast corner of the roof for the fifth time, she paused and lowered her book.

Khalid held his breath, as he watched her stoop next to the clay pot. When she stood up, he could see the paper in her hand. She stared at it a long time before placing it in the flyleaf of her book. She gazed up at the sky for a moment and then looked over towards his house. Khalid stepped out from behind the palm. The two stared at each other for what seemed like a millennium to him before she turned away and descended to the courtyard of her house.

* * *

Khalid was weary and irritable when he returned from school that afternoon. The month of fasting had taken its toll and he was badly in need of a nap before resuming his homework. Even before he reached his house, the sound of a woman's wailing and keening assaulted him. As the eldest son, he would inevitably be drawn into the drama which he dreaded.

When he entered the house, he was surprised to see his aunt and uncle seated with his parents in the main room. His aunt, Umm Laila, was rocking back and forth in her chair, her hands covering her head. His mother attempted to comfort her.

"*Haram! Haram!*" the woman cried, ignoring his mother's ministrations.

Khalid's father gestured for him to join them.

"What has happened?" Khalid asked with a glance at his hysterical aunt.

"Our daughter has shamed us. Shamed the family," Abu Laila replied, tears standing in his dark eyes. "Her mother found a letter in Laila's school book this morning. It was from a boy."

Khalid felt his blood turn to ice despite the summer heat. He looked down, afraid his eyes would betray him.

"She claims she does not know how the letter came to be in her book, or who would put it there," Abu Laila continued. "I've beaten her, and her mother has cut off her hair, but her answer does not change.

The remainder of the conversation was lost on Khalid. The ringing in his ears drowned out all sound. When his uncle and aunt finally left, his father sent for coffee.

"What will happen to her?" Khalid asked his father.

Shaking his head, his father replied, "She will be withdrawn from school and kept in the house until an appropriate marriage can be arranged. She has always been a modest girl. Her father believes she is telling the truth, but he cannot take that chance. I would not."

Khalid remained in his bed that night and did not go up to the roof. He thought of how close he had come to disaster and shuddered. He wondered why she kept her silence. He pictured her lovely face bruised and swollen, her head shorn of its glorious hair. Why?

After a week of excruciating fear, Khalid relaxed and determined his deed was safe from discovery. He'd had time to ponder the situation. Laila had enticed him with her eyes that first night, against all the edicts of modesty. He was now convinced she knew all along he was watching her on the roof. She paraded back and forth pretending to read only to tease him. And he had been fool enough to be drawn into her web. She remained silent to cover her own guilt as she should.

In a month's time, Khalid would leave for Germany and a new life. His father had slaughtered a lamb, and Khalid had proudly stepped across the carcass for luck. The family celebrated with a feast. His mother and aunt, along with their daughters, prepared buttered rice sweetened with cinnamon and raisins, stuffed grape leaves, fried *kibbee*, and an array of salads. Honey drenched baklava followed with Turkish coffee.

Khalid only caught a glimpse of Laila, who did not leave the kitchen. She wore a shapeless black shift, and her head was covered with a scarf. Her slender shoulders hunched forward, and she kept her head bent to her task.

Chapter Fifteen

Decatur, GA

Dr. Edward Firth, Sami's immediate superior, had recently been appointed. A respected scientist, he was also a talented politician, an impeccable man with a thatch of graying hair, a firm jaw, and a thin, aquiline nose. He stood up, smiling, and held out his hand when Sami entered the office.

Sitting down again behind his desk, Firth gestured Sami to accept a chair upholstered in green leather. He didn't interrupt as Sami told him about the perceived threat but listened with a concerned frown. His hands remained folded atop his desk which was littered with books and stacks of papers as though he were still unpacking. But the wall behind him displayed an array of diplomas and photos of himself posing with other dignitaries.

"Has the man threatened you directly?" Firth asked.

Sami considered. "Not directly," he answered, "but I consider his appearance in my office and his reference to my family a threat."

"It is difficult to deal with a perceived threat without some evidence." Firth sat back in his chair and studied Sami with steady blue eyes. "You say he mentioned Dugway Proving Ground. That's in Salt Lake City, where they test military weapons. Are you aware of any scheduled shipment?"

"No," said Sami, "I'm not involved in that area."

"Do you have any idea why this person would have singled you out?" continued Firth, his gaze remaining on Sami's face.

Sami thought before answering. "I suppose because I am a Muslim, and he thinks I would be sympathetic." He thought about his brother in Ramallah, but decided against revealing that information. Something about Firth made him uncomfortable. He suspected the man was questioning his credibility.

Rising from his chair, Firth crossed the room to a tall window. He rubbed his chin as he looked down over the campus. Two girls shared a bench, their heads bent over their iPhones. Oversized backpacks rested at their feet. A scuttle of leaves drifted down from huge old trees as the wind rattled their branches and breathed a hint of approaching autumn.

Turning back to Sami he said, "I will have someone look into this, but the information must stay confidential. We can't afford a witch hunt or a media driven panic."

"Of course," Sami agreed.

"It goes without saying that any shipment from here is very well protected, but we do need to be vigilant," Firth continued, coming back to stand behind his desk. "I appreciate your bringing this to my attention, Dr. Nasser. We will check it out."

Firth watched the door close after Sami. He picked up his Mont Blanc and studied it absently, rolling it over in his fingers. *What to do?*

"A handsome and intelligent young man," he mused, "and an interesting, if ill-timed, story. It could be genuine. But it could also be a ploy to retain dollars for bioterrorism." He picked up the phone receiver and punched in a number.

"Ted, how are you? Listen, I'm trying to get my bearings here with the personnel. Can you provide me with some background information? I'd appreciate it. His name is Dr. Sami Nasser."

Chapter Sixteen

The Ritz Carlton, Arlington, VA

Sami nursed a crystal glass of single malt and tried to look interested as the speaker droned away.

"The Jimmy and Rosalynn Carter Award for Humanitarian Contributions to the Health of Human Kind is presented by the National Foundation for Infectious Diseases to individuals whose outstanding humanitarian efforts and achievements have contributed significantly to improving the health of humankind."

There was a polite burst of applause from the audience, clustered around tables adorned with white linen cloths. Candles flickered between the centerpieces of white mums, yellow lilies, and lacy ferns. The dimmed chandeliers threw the stage into a pool of light.

Sami had heard it all before. He did admire Dr. Berner, for his intellect and dedication. But like Carter himself, the man was hopelessly naïve. A common, if not fatal, failing in the West.

He looked across the table at his wife. She smiled back at him. The candlelight illuminated her green eyes seductively. Her beauty made his heart clench. The long dark hair was swept back from her face which accentuated her cheekbones and graceful neck. Growing up in a loving and privileged family, she had no idea of the evil that existed throughout the world. Her innocence was one of the things that made him fall in love with her. Now it frightened him. How could he protect her and their daughter? The evil was no longer intangible. It was coiled on his doorstep.

Karen was surprised to see Sami order another scotch. He seldom drank, and then usually a single cocktail. His dismissal of her concern only heightened her fear that he was shutting her out. It had to do with the strange young man whose eyes had burned into her during the brief encounter at Sami's office. Never in her life had she experienced such venom from another human being.

She glanced at Dr. Moussa Hayek and his wife seated at the next table. Cultured and gracious, it was hard for her to imagine they would have such a nephew. As she watched, Nawal Hayek whispered in her husband's ear and then rose and headed in the direction of the powder room. Karen winked at Sami and motioned towards the same direction. She was unaware of his gaze following her until she disappeared from sight.

The ladies room was dimly lit and decorated in hues of brown. Karen scanned the room and noticed only two of the stalls appeared occupied. She crossed to the bay of ceramic bowl sinks set in black granite. A tall snowy orchid sprouting from an amethyst colored glass vase arched over the corner sink where Karen stopped and checked her appearance in the mirror. The simple black cocktail dress was set off by a matching string of pearls and stud earrings. After applying a dash of pale rose lipstick, she set down her evening bag and pumped an ivory glob of liquid soap into her hand. A contemporary stainless spigot controlled the water, and she manipulated it until the temperature was comfortable. She took her time massaging in the soap, as she watched the doors behind her in the mirror.

A toilet flushed and a middle-aged woman, wearing an emerald green dress with a short beaded jacket, emerged from the middle stall. She gave Karen a smile and nod as she headed to the sink on the other end. Another toilet flushed, and Nawal came out of the next stall, smoothing her skirt of navy-blue satin. She selected the sink next to Karen as the woman in green finished drying her hands on a linen towel and left the room.

Nawal was very pretty, with glossy black hair and a wide expressive mouth. It curved into a smile when her eyes met Karen's in the mirror over the sink.

"This is an attractive faucet but strange," she said with a laugh.

"Yes, and a little temperamental too," answered Karen. "You're Nawal Hayek, aren't you? I'm not sure you remember me. We met at a CDC conference last year. I'm Karen, my husband is Sami Nasser."

"Of course! How nice to see you again." Moussa speaks often of Sami and his talents."

"That's very kind. Sami does the same. He's excited to be working with your husband on the new program."

They both turned off the water and selected towels from the oblong stainless holder sitting between them.

"I believe I met your nephew recently at Sami's office. Is he here for a visit?"

Nawal looked puzzled as she crumpled her towel and dropped it into a basket under the vanity. "We have no family in the U.S. at this time. Perhaps you confused the name?"

"Oh, I must have misunderstood Sami," said Karen discarding her own towel and retrieving her black brocade evening bag. She smiled again as she held the door open for Nawal.

Sami's eyes tracked her to the table. His gaze was opaque and inscrutable, and he was no longer smiling. She looked down at her plate and the half empty glass of champagne. He was the liar, so why did she feel the blood rising in her cheeks? She finally looked up to meet his gaze. He knew that she knew.

Chapter Seventeen

Sami inspected the impressive bar in their hotel room and selected a bottle of Macallan 12. Setting the bottle on the gleaming granite, he shrugged out of his jacket and pulled off his bow tie. He studied himself in the mirror behind the bar. Pulling off his tie and loosening his collar, he exposed the golden brown of his upper chest, a pleasing contrast against the white silk. His focus shifted to the bottle in front of him, a slight smile tweaking his lips. The ice bucket was full, surrounded by crystal glasses. "Very hospitable," he murmured. Scooping up a handful of cubes, Sami enjoyed the tinkle as they hit the glass. He poured the amber liquid slowly, relishing the clean scent and anticipating the first burning swallow.

The bathroom door clicked open, and a yellow shaft of light crawled across the carpet. Sami turned and stared at Karen, framed in the doorway. Her slender body, clad in a thin cotton nightgown, was backlit and exposed. The gown hid nothing from him.

"Can I get you something?" he asked, turning back to his drink but studying her reflection in the mirror.

Karen hesitated just a moment. "Champagne, if they have it." Entering the room, her nakedness was at once swathed and hidden from view. She settled on a small velveteen stool in front of the vanity and removed several artfully placed barrettes. An abundance of dark hair tumbled down to frame her shoulders. In the subdued light, it shone a rich deep brown with hints of chestnut.

Sami came up behind her and set the flute of chilled Veuve Clicquot down on the vanity. His retracting hand brushed her shoulder and paused there. His fingers caught the luxuriant mass of her hair which he twisted and then pulled aside. Setting down his glass, he ran a cool damp index finger along the nape of her neck. Karen felt the silken hairs rise on her arms. She reached for the champagne flute and admired the bubbling liquid before taking a swallow. Her bottle green eyes narrowed when they met his in the mirror. "You're drunk," she stated.

"I am indeed." His hand was gently massaging the nape of her neck.

"Mmmmm," Karen arched her body and let her head fall back, exposing the long creamy column of her neck.

Setting down his glass, Sami knelt beside her and brushed his lips along the side of her ear, flicking his tongue across the lobe. "*Habibti*," he whispered.

Sami's head dropped to her lap, his hands easing down along her hips and legs as she clutched fistfuls of his dark curls. Gently kneading her calves, he worked his way up to her thighs. When he brushed the core of her warmth, she trembled and opened herself like a flower unfolding. He leaned back and tugged at the buttons on his shirt. She helped him pull it over his head and then held up her arms so he could remove her nightgown.

He rose to his feet and allowed her to unbuckle his belt and pull down his trousers. He moaned when she took him in her mouth as her hands caressed his buttocks and the back of his thighs. "I can't wait," his voice was hoarse.

Karen looked up, her eyes darkened with desire. Lifting her in his arms, Sami carried her to the bed where the covers were already drawn back. She reached up to encircle his neck and draw him down. Parting her lips with his tongue, he tasted himself. Her body strained upward, and she wrapped her legs around his waist. He held back as long as he could until she begged for release.

* * *

Sami refreshed his drink and poured Karen another glass of champagne. She lay across the rumpled bed on her stomach, watching him. When he came and sat beside her, she rolled over, propping herself against the pillows. He was always amazed at how unselfconscious she was about her body. It was completely alien to his own culture where nudity was shameful, especially for a woman. At these moments he felt as if they were in a cocoon, buffered from the rest of the world and its miseries.

He handed her the flute, as she nestled up against him. "Thank you, sir," she murmured, a smile playing on her exquisite lips. He raised his brows in acknowledgment.

"I might need a cigarette," he responded, causing her to throw back her head and laugh. She took a sip of champagne and rolled it around in her mouth, enjoying the hint of grapefruit. Resting her head on his shoulder, she sighed.

"Can you tell me about it?" Karen asked, keeping her eyes down.

"No." Sami replied, and felt her body stiffen. He turned her face up to meet his. Her eyes were clear and wide now as she regarded him.

"Do you trust me?" he asked, softly.

She nodded, never taking her eyes from his face, "Yes."

"I hate to leave you tomorrow," Karen continued. "Are you sure there is no way you can come with Mira and me?"

"I hate for you to leave, but I'll join you as soon as I can," Sami replied, running his hand along her firm, lightly tanned thigh. "Besides, absence makes the heart grow fonder."

"And hornier," she murmured and gasped as his hand moved upward.

Chapter Eighteen

Savannah, GA

"Hey girl, it's your biggest fan," Karen smiled into the phone.

"Hey yourself," Sarah quipped. The Savannah artist, who was Karen's former roommate from college, couldn't hide her delight. "Does this mean you're coming to my exhibit?"

"What do you think?" Karen asked. "Your invitations were impressive, very snooty patootie. Do I need to bring a long dress?"

"Give me a break," Sarah responded. "You'd look stunning in a potato sack, and you know it."

Karen ignored the compliment. "I'll expect a sneak preview, and I want first crack at buying a painting."

"Whoa, you got it. Two are already sold and one reserved, but there are plenty more. When will you be here?"

"Mira and I are coming to Haig Point to see my parents on Tuesday. Could we meet for lunch or dinner on Wednesday?"

"Mmm, let me look," Sarah shuffled through the dog-eared date book she had retrieved from her desk. "Lunch will work," she said. "So you're not bringing the handsome hubby?"

"He may come later in the week. Up to his ears in work as usual," Karen responded. She hoped he would make it in time for the exhibit on Saturday night. Maybe have dinner at 700 Drayton and a night at the Mansion on Forsyth Park. She felt her face flush.

"It will be fun to have some girl time," Karen told Sarah.

"Yes, reminisce on those halcyon days at Vanderbilt."

Sarah wrinkled her nose. "Are we getting old or what?"

"Don't even go there," Karen said. "Wait until you see Mira. She is growing before my eyes. Is there any chance you could come to Haig for a day?"

Sarah ran a hand through her short-cropped red hair. "My schedule is really crazy getting ready for the show, but I'll try."

"I promise I won't take you to Swampside Mary's," Karen added.

"Good God," Sarah groaned, "The porta-potty palace. I'd forgotten about that place. Wasn't that where your mom got sick and hurled her gumbo?"

"Please," Karen begged, "I've tried to erase that scene from my memory." She closed her eyes for a moment, and vividly recalled her elegant mother leaning over the railing on the restaurant deck, her face ashen and contorted while her father stood by, helpless for one of the few times in his life.

"Weren't there a couple of mangy dogs that hung around?" Sarah continued. "And a huge pig or a hog...whatever you call it."

"Ned," Karen offered. "The restaurant mascot and resident drunk. He's still there. And the place is still my father's favorite hangout. Go figure."

Sarah caught her reflection in the hallway mirror across from her. Crazy hair, she thought and made a face.

"You make me laugh," she told Karen. "And I needed that."

Karen paused, "I know, me too."

* * *

Sarah stared at the phone for a while. How could she have doubted that Karen would come? She was the closest friend Sarah had ever had. At one time, she had wished for a deeper relationship. How could she not have been attracted to someone as blessed by the gods as her former roommate? If Karen was aware, she never let it show.

The two had been flung together their first year at Vanderbilt. Sarah was skinny and sullen, her face a mass of freckles, and her hair an unruly mop of red curls. Her mother had escorted her to college but fled gratefully after the first day. Her father, as usual, was busy in Washington working hard with the other senators to keep their personal slush fund rolling in. Screw them both!

Karen had breezed in wearing cutoff jeans and looking like she stepped off the cover of Vogue. Her parents were right out of a fifties sitcom; Ward and June Cleaver. They descended on Sarah like the plague, complimenting the hideous bedspread her mother had bought, offering to help unpack, inviting her to dinner. Karen, at least, was smart enough to keep her mouth shut. It was hate at first sight.

The roommates drew up a schedule ensuring they would avoid each other as much as possible, and the first few weeks passed uneventful. But Sarah returned one night, to find Karen curled up on the ratty cushion that served as a window seat. She was gazing out at the gloom with a book perched on her lap.

"I thought this was my night in," Sarah quipped, dumping her shoulder bag on the bed.

Karen turned towards her. She was wearing an oversized gray sweater and black leggings. Her hair was pulled starkly back from her face, and her feet were bare.

"God she has amazing eyes!" thought Sarah.

"It's raining and I'm tired of the library," Karen replied. "Why do you hate me so much?"

Sarah rolled her eyes and hunched out of her jean jacket. She ran her hands through her thick hair which the humidity had transformed into a medusa's crown of flaming ringlets that snaked out in riotous disarray.

"Do we need to do this tonight?" she asked. "I've had a really shitty day."

"It's a simple question," returned Karen. She rearranged her long legs so she was sitting Indian style facing the room. She kept her eyes on her roommate's face.

Sarah plopped down on her bed. "I don't hate you," she said meeting Karen's gaze. "I just think we're not really compatible."

"How would you know?" Karen asked. "We've barely said ten words to each other."

"Why does it matter to you?"

"I saw some of your paintings displayed in the art room. I liked them, and I think it's sad I don't know anything about you."

"Are you an artist?"

"No. I appreciate art and am interested in art history but I have no talent."

Sarah had a bemused expression on her face. "What else do you like?" she asked.

"Writing," Karen replied. "I like to think I have some talent there. And reading."

"What do you read?"

"Almost anything except romance and science fiction. What about you?"

"Mysteries or crime novels with lots of mayhem and sex."

"Thomas Harris," Karen responded, pointing a finger at Sarah.

"Love him," Sarah flashed a quick smile and raised her eyebrows. "I guess we might have a few things in common. You win."

"You didn't tell me much about yourself," Karen responded.

"I'm going to be a famous artist. That's it." Sarah got up from the bed and stretched, suppressing a yawn. "If you don't need the bathroom, I'm going to take a quick shower."

"Go ahead," said Karen with a wave of her hand. After the bathroom door closed, she turned back to the window. It would be an interesting friendship.

Chapter Nineteen

Chamblee, GA

Khalid glanced at the clock on the kitchenette wall of the rented room he shared with his two companions. It was almost time for the midday prayer. He looked at Mahmoud who slouched on a stained maroon sofa that also served as a bed.

Much as Khalid disliked the big man, he had to acknowledge his competence. He had put both Mahmoud and Abdullah to the test on the first night they arrived. The cab driver, Abdul Al-Awan, had been summoned to drive Mahmoud to a location in downtown Atlanta.

Mahmoud slid into the back seat of the cab and in the rear view mirror, saw the man's narrow dark eyes flick back at him. "Is it okay to smoke?" Mahmoud asked in Arabic, as he watched the man pull away from the curb.

"Not really," Al-Awan replied glancing at the no smoking sign, "But I can open the windows." The big man made him nervous. He had entered the cab with a black gym bag which now sat on the floor. The majority of passengers left bags or parcels on the seat beside them.

Mahmoud lit up a cigarette and asked, "Do you smoke?"

The driver hesitated a moment before responding, "*Aiwa.*"

Smiling, Mahmoud passed his cigarette to Al-Awan and then lit another for himself, noting the post card of Mecca tucked behind a photo ID on the driver's visor. A string of plastic amber-colored prayer beads sporting a forlorn little tassel, swung from the mirror.

"I was not told there would be another assignment," said Al-Awan, blowing a puff of smoke out the driver's side window. The muggy night air assaulted him after the air conditioning, but it was worth the discomfort.

Mahmoud shrugged. "I am just a messenger. Like you brother, I do as I am told. How long have you been here?"

"Too long," Al-Awan sighed. "I came here to save money for my family and then return. Another year or two, *Inshallah*, I will go home."

"You have your own family? Children?" Mahmoud had settled back in the seat, one long leg stretched out to the side, his arm resting on the frame of the open window. He scanned the approaching skyscrapers and streets pulsing with neon.

Al-Awan smiled for the first time. "Yes, two boys."

"May Allah protect them," Mahmoud responded. "Where is home? You sound Syrian."

"Yes," said Al-Awan, relaxing his grip on the steering wheel and taking another drag from his cigarette. "I am from Damascus. What about you, brother?"

"Beriut," Mahmoud answered.

Al-Awan felt the hairs rise on the back of his neck. There was little love lost between the Syrians and the Lebanese. He tossed his half-smoked cigarette out the window. "Just ahead is your location," he said.

The car eased over to the curb on a dark street in Techwood Homes, a tenement just south of the Georgia Tech campus. A black sedan pulled up behind and shut off its lights.

Al-Awan looked out the windshield and in the gutter ahead saw a crumpled fast food bag and a squashed paper cup illuminated by his headlights. A balmy wind rustled leaves in the tree above him and a few fluttered down to land on the hood of his car.

Mahmoud shifted in the seat behind him and Al-Awan squeezed his eyes shut. "Please, please..." he begged. The silencer was cold against the back of his head, and he smelled the cigarette smoke on the man's breath as he whispered in his ear.

"Today you shall enter Paradise."

The two muffled shots were barely audible to the car behind him. Mahmoud leaned into the front seat and removed the driver's wallet from his pocket. He used a white handkerchief to wipe the surfaces he had touched and stepped out of the car. Swiping the door handle, he scanned the street to insure it was still empty. Khalid and Abdullah pulled up beside him, and he ducked into the back seat.

* * *

Khalid was pleased. Two days after the incident, the local news stated there were no leads, and the murder was attributed most likely to gang members. He pulled out a cigarette then tossed the pack to Mahmoud.

"Have you anything to report?" he asked.

Mahmoud shrugged as he fished out the last fag and crumpled the package. "She goes shopping and jogs and does errands, like the other days. Why are we watching her?"

"It's not your concern," Khalid snapped. "You follow orders, just as I do."

Striking a match with his thumb, Mahmoud shrugged again. He had large hands. At six feet three inches, he would have towered over Khalid, but he remained seated. Above his lanky body, the handsome face wore an open expression that was disarmingly boyish. He inhaled deeply, considering his response, and then exhaled.

"I think she might be preparing for a trip."

Khalid stared at him through the bluish plume of smoke.

"I saw her filling the back of her car with packages, bags, golf clubs...things like that," Mahmoud continued, gesturing with his cigarette.

"You fool!" Khalid exploded, jumping out of his chair. "When did you see this? If we lose the wife and the girl..."

Mahmoud put up his hands. "Wait, wait," he soothed. "Abdullah is watching her. If there is any change, he will call. They are never out of our sight."

Khalid was pacing now, "I don't trust this doctor, and I don't trust his wife. If she goes anywhere, you and Abdullah will follow her. Do you understand?" he demanded.

"Of course," Mahmoud affirmed, flicking his ash onto the floor.

"This should have been done by now." Khalid fumed. "The doctor is unreasonable. He has been poisoned by that *sharmuta*." He stopped pacing and confronted Mahmoud. "Do you know that she looked me full in the face? She flaunts her beauty with no shame instead of saving it for her husband."

"She is beautiful," Mahmoud agreed. In truth, he found many of the infidel women attractive. He was shocked at their openness but not offended by it. Previously, his contact with the West had been through charity organizations working in the slums of Beirut. The females were mostly plain and many past their prime. The images in movies and magazines were surreal and untouchable. Not so the women he encountered in Atlanta. They smiled at him, their eyes bright with invitation.

Khalid made a sound of disgust, as he ground out his cigarette stub in an overflowing ashtray. He closed his eyes and rubbed the bridge of his nose. He was sick to death of this place. Everything, from the dusty red drapes to the faux leather furniture, offended him. Indeed everything in the corrupt Western World was offensive, except maybe the cigarettes.

Chapter Twenty

Hilton Head Island, SC

Karen pulled into the parking lot of the Haig Point embarkation center on Hilton Head Island. Mira had slept for much of the trip but was now wide awake, her brown eyes glistening with excitement. She clutched a bag of her favorite books and cradled a plastic Pegasus, its purple mane spilling over her slender arm.

Their luggage was efficiently loaded into grey plastic tubs by the staff. Mira hesitated before dropping her satchel into one of the waiting tubs, but clung to the horse. "Pegasus has to ride with us," she stated emphatically.

"That sounds like a good plan Missy Mira." The tall woman's face split into a grin so the gold rimming her front teeth flashed in the sun. Karen returned the smile, "Hello Lizzie. How have you been?"

"Not bad. Season's almost over. Your momma and daddy will be happy to see you two." Lizzie replied. "Is Dr. Nasser coming?" She was a tall strong woman and hefted the bags with ease.

"He had to work," Mira replied, "but he might come later." She was prancing Pegasus along the railing that led to the shuttle boat. "I told him he would miss the crabs. Will your momma bring us crabs?"

Lizzie threw back her head and laughed, sending her long thicket of braids bobbing. "Oh you know she will honey! We went crabbing this past weekend and caught a mess."

"How is your mother?" Karen asked.

"Oh, ornery as ever; she's a tough old woman. You'll see her around." She paused with one broad hand shading her eyes, and looked at Karen. "Are you all right honey?"

Karen reached out and squeezed the woman's arm. The feel of her warm solid flesh was reassuring. As a child, she had imagined Lizzie to be an African princess, majestic, graceful, and kind. "I'm fine. A little tired, but fine." Her eyes scanned the horizon for Daufuskie Island, shimmering green in the distance. "This always feels like coming home," she added.

Turning back to her daughter she said, "Do you want to come with me to park the car?"

"Pegasus wants to stay here with Lizzie," Mira replied, scooting up next to her friend.

Lizzie laughed and put a hand on the little girl's shoulder. "You go on. Missy Mira can help me out here."

Karen finally found an empty parking spot in the last row of the lot that backed up against a pine forest. She checked the backseat one more time to be sure she hadn't left anything and locked the car with her key fob. Clutching her oversized purse and eager to be on the shuttle boat, she sprinted back to the embarkation center.

* * *

The two Arabs watched Karen as she unloaded her luggage. A tall black woman approached and greeted her warmly. This interested them. It did not fit what they had been told about Americans in the South. Karen then left her little girl with the black woman while she meandered up and down the aisles of the parking lot in her car before pulling in to a spot on the last aisle that was backed by forest.

They hunched down in the front seat of their sedan when she emerged from the silver Lexus, but Karen didn't glance in their direction. Abdullah smiled, making his lean dark face look feral. *"Allahu Akbar!"* he murmured. "God has led her to this spot."

Mahmoud nodded and punched open the glove box, pulling out the tracking device.

"Wait," said Abdullah. "You must approach from trees in front of her car so no one will see. I will warn you if anyone approaches." Mahmoud nodded again, and glanced around once more before exiting the car. He was glad for a chance to move about after the long drive. He was weary of inaction.

"I do not like it that she goes to the island without us," grumbled Abdullah, when Mahmoud returned to the car.

The tall man leaned back in his seat and sighed. "We have been through this. The shuttle boat is the only way on and off the island, and one must be a member to have access. You were with me when we inquired." He pointed at the embarkation center building for emphasis.

"We should tell Khalid," Abdullah insisted. "He told us to keep her in sight. What if she leaves the island by another boat?" he added.

"Then she will come to get her car, and we will follow her. You worry too much my friend."

Mahmoud turned on the screen and verified the tracking device. "You see," he said, causing Abdullah to grunt begrudgingly.

"We should get something to eat while we have time," Mahmoud continued. "She will not return soon."

Reluctantly, Abdullah backed out of his parking space, and cast a long look at the silver Lexus. He had a bad feeling as they drove toward downtown Hilton Head, but he could think of no rational argument to make.

Chapter Twenty One

As they approached the southern tip of Daufuskie Island, Karen sought out the lighthouse. Built in 1873, it underwent an extensive restoration in 1984 using original floor plans and other historic reference material. The inside was furnished with period antiques. She and Sami had spent their honeymoon there, and she smiled when she recalled Lizzie's horror.

"Did you see any spirits?" the woman had asked, narrowing her eyes.

Karen had laughed. "No, but I hoped we might have been visited by Maggie's ghost." She recalled reading the lighthouse keeper's account penned on October 22, 1882.

"I resolved to compensate myself somewhat for the lonely week that had passed and saddled the old mule and struck out for Haig Point Lighthouse. The day was fine and I enjoyed the ride very much. Was kindly received by Lighthouse Keeper Mr. Comer and his wife. We sat and talked for some little time and was most pleasantly surprised by the entrance of a lovely young lady wearing sweet perfume, Miss Maggie the daughter of the old folks."

Unfortunately Miss Maggie had died in a fall from the tower a few years earlier.

"I wouldn't go near that place." said Lizzie, rolling her eyes at the newlyweds.

As they approached the island, Karen was jarred back to the present. She took her daughter out onto the upper deck where they inspected the elegant homes lining the beach road, buffered from the ocean by a strip of wetlands. Mother and daughter laughed as they watched pelicans dive bombing for fish.

"Dolphin!" the little girl yelled, jumping up and down as she pointed. And indeed there was a pod gliding and humping alongside the boat.

Being here made Karen feel like a child again. The population had grown in the past few years, and many more residences lined the beach and dotted the golf course. But the roads were still free of cars. Towering live oaks stood as timeless sentinels. And the ghosts remained, haunting the old cemeteries and the tabby house ruins built from oyster shells to house the slaves.

Karen and her daughter spotted Alice, as the boat slid into the dock. A slender, pretty woman, she carried her age well. "There's Nana!" yelled Mira, dropping her winged horse so she could wave with both arms. "I don't see Papa." She stopped suddenly, her brows drawing together.

Karen retrieved the discarded Pegasus and reached for Mira's hand. "Don't worry sweetie. He is probably out catching crabs to surprise us for dinner." But she searched the dock again for her father's lanky frame. She needed him.

Chapter Twenty Two

Daufuskie Island, SC

Karen stood on the broad front porch of her parents' home and waved as her mother and daughter took off in their golf cart heading for the pool. Mira grinned and waved back. She was thrilled to be riding in the front seat with her feet propped up on an enormous beach bag stuffed with towels, lotion, snacks and toys. The pool overlooked the beach, and Karen knew the afternoon would include a seashell hunt. She remembered trolling the same beach as a child, clambering over the mountains of white oyster shells and marveling at the sight of a hermit crab scuttling along the water's edge.

She had arranged to have a golf cart of her own so she could drive to meet her father on the west end of the island. The wild end. She smiled, recalling her mother's irritation when she related that Karen's father was at Swampside Mary's with his cronies. Alice couldn't fathom how her husband, previously the head of Neurology at Emory, could possibly have anything in common with the islanders outside the exclusive enclave of Haig Point.

"I can't understand what draws him to that place," Alice said. "It's a dump, the food is awful, and that hideous pig!" She gave a small shiver of revulsion.

Mira immediately picked up on "that pig". "Ned!" she shrieked. "I want to see Ned!" It took both Karen and her mother to convince the child that Ned would be sleeping in the noon heat, and the pool would be much more fun for now. Tomorrow would be a better time to visit Ned. Karen knew they would have to make the visit before Sami arrived. He was not a practicing Muslim but he drew the line at a three-hundred pound beer guzzling pig that was the restaurant mascot.

Karen had always been close to her father. In retirement, John Cameron transferred his brilliance and passion from the miracle of the human brain to the fragile ecosystem on Daufuskie. When her parents first retired, her father lasted a month on the golf circuit. Always a naturalist and history buff, he was fascinated by every aspect of the island and the people who had inhabited it for generations.

While Alice busied herself with golf, bridge, and local charitable organizations, John roamed the island, fished in the Calibogue Sound for trout and redfish and in the interior ponds for bass. He sought out the local fisherman who taught him how to cast a net for shrimp. More important, they showed him where to cast.

Fascinated by the local Gullah culture, John joined with local leaders who hoped to restore homes and other historic buildings to keep the island from drowning in a sea of residential developments. Through Lizzie, he formed a tentative friendship with her mother, Louise, who taught him how to catch crabs and how to prepare them along with dirty rice and gumbo. She would never fully trust a white person, but the two shared a fierce love of the islands.

Louise had grown up on the neighboring Bull Island and moved to Daufuskie with her husband, Daryl, to work in the booming oyster industry. At the time, oystering was the only means to earn a living other than cotton and vegetable farming. Daufuskie oysters were world famous for their quality.

Unfortunately, the oyster business was given a deadly blow in the 1950's when industrialization came to nearby Savannah, polluting the Savannah River and contaminating the oyster beds. Many of the locals left for jobs on the mainland but others, like Louise and Daryl, clung stubbornly to their island homes. He had died several years ago, and Louise was alone now, except for Lizzie who routinely spent her days off crabbing alongside her mother.

Karen unplugged her golf cart and dumped her bag on the seat next to her. She'd brought sun screen, bug spray, and several bottles of water. She opened one and took a long swig, then plopped it into a drink holder. She backed carefully out of the small garage that also housed bicycles, fishing rods, and golf clubs. Wincing at the shrill signal emitted when the cart was in reverse, she was relieved to switch into forward gear.

Pulling onto the road, she floored the accelerator pedal and noted the lack of response. Unlike her parents privately owned carts, the rentals had governors installed to restrict the speed. She supposed it was to protect golfers who over-imbibed during the game. Karen smiled as she remembered her father's story about taking a group of tipsy golfers out at night to supposedly look for deer. He led them to the center of Haig Point, turned out his light and drove home, leaving them to drive in circles through the labyrinth of lanes and courts and drives in the dark. There were no street lamps, and the huge trees blocked out much of the night sky. After an hour or so, John took pity and set out to rescue them.

Karen had ridden her bicycle throughout the compound since childhood and knew every inch. She tooled down Haig Point Road passing Night Heron Court, Marsh Lake Lane, and River Marsh Run. During long ago summers, she would follow these roads to their end and then cut through the forest to reach the portion of the island that faced the Cooper River. At that time there was nothing but a single community dock and mountains of bleached oyster shells along the water. She dubbed it her secret beach. The land had been sold since then and palatial homes now sprawled amidst the wetlands; their private docks stretched far out over the water.

The Equestrian Center rose up on her right. A few

horses were in the paddock, clustered in a spot of shade, their tails twitching to chase the flies. Another cart had stopped and two children were trying to entice the animals with a handful of carrots. Karen smiled and waved as she passed, then continued through the gate, exiting the compound onto Old Haig Point Road. Now she was in the "authentic" part of the island that had always captivated her. The towering vegetation, teeming with cawing birds and humming insects, closed in on both sides. While the golf cart rumbled along, she searched for what the locals called "oyster homes" set back from the road. The tin roofs were rusted on most, their foundations deteriorating. Many had doors and windows painted bright blue to ward off witches and wandering spirits.

Karen recalled Sami's fascination the first time he visited Daufuskie during their engagement. The practice of using blue to protect against evil dated back to ancient Egypt and, according to him, was still very much alive in the Middle East. It struck her that despite his cosmopolitan demeanor, the Arab heritage remained very much a part of his identity.

A horn blared in back of her, jolting Karen out of her reverie. She quickly pulled over to the side of the road as a dilapidated pick-up truck careened past her. Trucks and cars were allowed outside the gates of Haig Point. What if it had stopped? She was in the middle of nowhere without a sign of another human being. She had never been afraid as a child wandering the island, but the tangled green wilderness suddenly seemed sinister. She was glad Swampside Mary's was just up ahead.

* * *

Relief washed over Karen with the salt breeze blowing in from the Calibogue Sound. She pulled her cart up next to John's signature blue Gem cart, wondering if the color was a nod to the locals' superstition. Knowing her father, it wouldn't surprise her.

In the low-country humidity, everything about Swampside Mary's drooped, from the battered tin roof to the enormous hog snoring under the porch. Crossing the wooden deck, Karen opened the sagging screen door and entered the bar. A pair of desultory ceiling fans pushed around the stifling air, but it felt good to be out of the sun. She pushed her dark glasses up so they sat atop her head and tucked back a few strands of hair that had escaped from her pony tail.

Karen immediately spotted her father perched on a bar stool and deep in conversation with a grizzled fisherman. They both turned to look when the door slammed shut behind her. John's sun-browned face cracked into a delighted grin.

"Kiddo!" he cried, opening his arms wide.

"Dad, I've missed you," she said, allowing herself to be wrapped in his familiar hug. "Why weren't you at the dock?" she added accusingly, though she knew full well the answer.

John eyed his daughter sheepishly. "You know how your mother is. She needs her time to cluck and fuss over you and Mira. Besides, I knew you'd come here." He winked and turned to his companion who appeared much younger up close.

"Look here, can you believe this beautiful woman is my daughter?"

"Oh Dad!" embarrassed, Karen made a face.

"Ma'am," the young man rose from his stool and slightly bowed his head. A network of fine lines framed turquoise eyes, startling in his bronze face. Thick dark hair fell across his forehead, and he sported several days' growth of beard.

"Karen, this is Nate, a tour guide on Bull Island," said her father. "He knows the name of every species that flies, crawls, or swims over there. And he's written a couple of books."

Nate smiled shyly, exposing an overlapping front tooth which was the only thing marring his rugged perfection.

"Really," Karen eyed him with renewed interest. "I've always wanted to go there. I heard it's one of the few untouched sanctuaries left."

"That it is," John agreed. "But you wouldn't want to go without a guide. The wild life is pretty much uncontrolled." From behind steel-rimmed glasses, his sharp grey eyes scrutinized her. "But I think you have other things on your mind." He nodded to his friend.

"If you'll excuse us Nate, we have some catching up to do."

"Of course, nice to meet you Ma'am," Nate replied. "Any time you would like a tour just let me know."

Karen smiled, "I would love that, thank you."

"My pleasure," Nate added. "Your dad is quite a legend around here." With the same slight bow of his head, he resumed his stool.

John had garnered two cold beers and now directed his daughter towards the door.

"See you later, Doc!" the bartender called. John raised his beer in a salute. Everyone on the island called him "Doc". In addition to being a term of respect, he was well known for removing an errant fishhook or two from a grateful islander or tourist.

John handed Karen a beer as they paused on the deck and let their eyes adjust to the brightness after the gloom. She pulled down the dark glasses, shielding her eyes.

"Everything looks the same," Karen remarked, surveying the familiar landscape. "Except the port-a-potties are gone. She gestured toward a small brick structure with a door on each side. "Are those real bathrooms?"

"Yes," her father replied, "Progress marches on. But you didn't come here to discuss indoor plumbing."

Karen became suddenly shy under his keen gaze. "Come on," he gestured, let's go out on the dock.

"Yes," she agreed, grateful for their silent communication. The panorama of water, sky, and reeling gulls generated a sense of peace inside Karen. She sighed and breathed deeply. "God, I love the smell!"

Her father nodded, gazing out over the sound. He took a sip of his beer and she did the same, delighting in the feel of the icy liquid on her tongue and the bitter tang.

"What's wrong Kiddo?" John asked, turning to face her.

Karen smiled. "Kiddo" had been her nickname since childhood, when she had shadowed her father and coveted his limited time away from Emory.

"I don't really know," she replied. "You haven't asked about Sami." John had been her husband's mentor which was how they had met. The two men were much alike, though her father was a hands-on physician while Sami buried himself in research.

"Is this about Sami?" Her father turned to her now. "Are you having problems?" She could read the dismay in his expression.

"No, no," she replied quickly. "It's nothing like that. There is something bothering him, and he won't confide in me. I know it has something to do with this awful man I met in his office last week. I just don't know what."

"What does Sami say?" her father asked.

"He originally claimed the man was a nephew of one of his colleagues, but I discovered that was a lie. When I confronted Sami, he just said he can't talk about it. He asked me to trust him."

John considered before responding. "You want my honest opinion?"

She nodded.

"You're over-reacting. I never set out to lie to your mother, but there were times I didn't share work experiences because I felt it would be a breach of privacy, or she might not understand the situation. Do you know if Sami has been having problems at work?"

"I know he is unhappy with the choice of the new director," she replied, "but he hasn't really elaborated on it. I'm not sure it's even work related. Lately he's been complaining about hostile looks from our neighbor. And he believes that several children didn't come to Mira's party because he's an Arab."

John shook his head. "I would hate to believe that, but prejudice has always existed. You knew when you married him there would be culture differences. Has Mira experienced any problems?"

"No, none," said Karen. "In fact, one of her new teachers is a Muslim. The kids all seem to adore her. You're probably right. I'm just being a worrywart. I get that from Mom you know."

"Do tell," John smiled. "I can't wait to see the little princess. Maybe I'll take her crabbing tomorrow."

"That would be great Dad. She'd love it! I would too, but I'm meeting Sarah over in Savannah for lunch. You remember Sarah?"

"Yes, of course, your artist friend from college. How is she doing?"

"She has an exhibition of her paintings set for next week at the Krona Gallery. Apparently it's a big deal."

"That's very impressive. I know the gallery, and they have some excellent works. She must be very good. Do you know what she paints?" John asked. He was a perfectionist and admired the trait in others.

"She used to do abstracts, but I got the impression she is experimenting with new concepts now. I'm really looking forward to a sneak preview," Karen replied, marveling at the breadth of her father's interests and knowledge.

"I am hoping she will come to Haig for a day. She really

wants to see Mira."

"That would be wonderful! We'd love to see her again. Please congratulate her for us and don't worry about Mira, I'll make sure she has fun." John winked at her for the second time that day.

"Oh I know you will." Karen laughed. "You may need to bring her by to see Ned. She made me promise."

"Ah Ned, poor sod," he said sadly. "Hasn't been doing so well lately. He may soon be going to that great pigsty in the sky." He looked up for emphasis and then drained his bottle.

Karen took a last long swallow. She considered asking if there would be a memorial pig roast but thought better of it. Both her father and daughter had an odd affinity for the beast. Sami, however, would be delighted by the news.

Karen linked arms with her father as they walked back to the restaurant. Chucking their empty bottles in a rusted old drum that served as a trash can, John asked Karen if she'd like another.

"Are you kidding?" she countered. "In this heat, I'd be under the table. I plan to save myself and raid your wine cellar tonight. I hope you have something decadent."

"Always," he beamed and she could see him mentally checking off the bottles he would recommend. Then he gave her a sly look. "Be careful what you say in front of your mother. She's afraid I'm squandering your inheritance on the grape."

This time it was Karen's turn to wink, co-conspirators to the end.

"I'm going to drive through Bloody Point on the way home. Want to join me?" she asked

"I need to finish up with Nate. We're working on a conservation proposal together. But you go ahead." He paused. "You might be surprised," he said. "It's gone downhill pretty fast this past year."

"So they haven't found a buyer?" she asked,

remembering the talk of bankruptcy last summer.

"Not that I know of," he replied. "But the point is still as beautiful as ever. Enjoy your drive. I'll be back in an hour or so."

"Okey-dokey," Karen gave her father a quick hug before climbing into her golf cart. "By the way, I love your new Gem car. Any special reason you picked blue?"

John stared at her, widening his eyes. "None at all," he replied. "You know I'm not superstitious."

"Uh huh," Karen smiled. "See you later."

John gave a brief wave as he watched his daughter drive off. Little clouds of dust swirled around the tires as she accelerated and headed around the bend. She looked so young with her hair pulled back and her face scrubbed clean, so much like her daughter, Mira. They possessed the same spirit too. He knew damn well Karen was not mollified by his dismissal of her fears.

Well, he would talk to his son-in-law. He was old enough to know that some things are easier settled between men. No doubt women felt the same way.

A disgruntled snort made him turn around to see Ned emerging from beneath the porch. Scuttling out backwards, with concerted effort, the enormous animal finally got to his feet. Swaying unsteadily, his beady little eyes blinked up at John.

"Well old sod, are you needing a drink? Come along then, we'll buy you a beer." With a second more emphatic snort, Ned lumbered after his patron.

Chapter Twenty Three

The golf cart shook and teetered as Karen drove along the back paths to Bloody Point. She knew all the short cuts by heart and had often delighted in driving visiting friends across the roughest terrain, while she pretended to be lost.

On a whim, she turned into a dirt track that meandered through the woods and ended at the only white cemetery on the island. Karen stopped her cart and got out. Someone had cleaned the headstones and cut back the vegetation. There were flowers on some graves. She wandered for a while, pausing to read the names and dates. Her heart clenched when she read the names of twin babies who died before their first year. It reminded her how fragile life was. She said a silent prayer for the souls of the dead before leaving and closing the wooden gate behind her.

Karen circled back to the main dirt road and soon entered the Bloody Point grounds. She had prepared herself, but the scene was much worse than she expected. The once lush grass on the golf course was withered and brown. The ponds where she had fished with her father were rancid with scum. Foot high clusters of weeds sprouted everywhere. The pool and clubhouse were closed, their parking lots in disrepair. How quickly the forest reclaimed its land. The thought made her shiver despite the heat. The homes along the water were magnificent as ever, but she wondered what it would be like to live amidst such ruin.

She finally reached the southern point of the island

which had been dubbed Bloody Point after the first English skirmish with Indians in 1715. According to lore, raiding Indians, at the behest of the Spanish, used the southern point on Daufuskie Island as a stopover to St. Augustine. On several occasions, the English surprised raiders on the point and killed all but a few who managed to escape.

Pulling her cart up to the forest edge, Karen parked beside the water. Despite its bloody history, this had always been her favorite place on the island. She bent down to a weathered gravestone and traced the letters, now barely legible. She could only make out the first name: Grace. The eulogy said she was born and died on Daufuskie. She'd been a little girl here, played in this same forest more than a century ago.

Grace had inhabited Karen's fantasy world as surely as the marauding Indians and English soldiers. Karen recalled being confused as a child when she learned there was only one white cemetery. The graves on Bloody Point all belonged to Gullahs. She knew if she had a choice, she would much prefer to be buried with them overlooking the water where there was always a clean breeze.

Absently scooping the dirt, she relived the hours spent searching for arrowheads. Sami had been delighted when she shared her childhood secrets. He confided his own experiences growing up in Ramallah, and though different, they were not completely alien.

"My mother told stories," he said. "Stories of the desert, with caliphs and princesses and magical beasts." He had laughed then. "My father never approved so she was careful to wait until he was away from the house. She would switch off the electricity and light a candle. We'd sit at her feet and watch the shadows on the wall, as she wove her tales. When my father returned, he would sniff around, and if he smelled candle wax we were in trouble."

Karen had been appalled at first. "How could your

mother live like that?"

Sami shrugged. "People make allowances for each other. Do you think your parents don't?" The question caught her off guard, and she had no answer.

She looked out over the water toward Tybee Island painted gold by the descending sun. Traces of purple and salmon marbled the dusk-blue sky, and Karen knew it was time to head home. She was suddenly anxious to see Mira, to hold her daughter and feel the baby-smooth skin against her face— to ward off the ghosts that wandered the night.

Chapter Twenty Four

Savannah, GA

Frowning at the mirror, Sarah Miles pulled at a spiky red prong of her gelled hair. She generally avoided mirrors but today she wanted to be at her best. As a soon-to-be-prominent artist, she was determined to look the part.

Turning away, she entered her workroom loft and surveyed the paintings lined up on the opposite wall. Sarah might never possess beauty, but she could appreciate it, and she could create it. She was anxious to see Karen's reaction.

When the doorbell rang, she crossed the small living portion of the apartment to the door and looked through the peephole. The concave lens distorted Karen's features, but she still looked perfect.

The two women were in each others' arms as soon as Sarah opened the door.

"I love this place!" said Karen, circling the room. The wide plank floors were scuffed and uneven with age but had a pleasing dark patina. The walls were painted a muted blue gray with cream woodwork that lightened the otherwise gloomy rooms. Simple sheers graced the long windows and the furniture was vintage flea market. An oversized antique desk, piled with books and correspondence, dominated one corner. Karen poked her head into the kitchen where a single wall contained a small electric stove, microwave, and fridge separated by a wood block counter. There was just enough room for a small round table and two rickety chairs.

"How old is this building?" Karen asked.

"Over a hundred years. You'd know it at night when the wind blows."

"I'll bet. We have the same problem with our house in Decatur, everything creaks. But I love that. What good is a house without a few ghosts?"

Sarah just shook her head.

"Okay, formalities aside. Where are they?" Karen asked, raising an arched brow.

Sarah flushed and gestured towards her studio. She'd paid to put in a sky-light that now illuminated her paintings. Karen's eyes scanned the spacious room cluttered with paints and drop cloths and a huge easel in the corner. She approached the paintings on the far wall and progressed slowly, standing close and then back as she inspected each canvas. Sarah watched while she bit a fingernail, then jerked her hand down in disgust. She'd been working on her nails for a month to make them presentable.

At last Karen came back to one painting. Two figures swirled across a muted background of blue and turquoise. Androgynous, their skin glowed deep bronze. One figure faced away, looking upward, while the other turned towards it, an arm beckoning.

"This is...amazing." Karen stammered. She looked at Sarah. "All of them," she encompassed the paintings with an expansive gesture, "I don't know what to say."

"God I hope you're right!" Sarah said. "When I think of the exhibition, I feel sick. I mean physically sick."

Karen quickly crossed over to her friend and hugged her. "Stop it! You know you're good. Let's discuss it over lunch. And maybe you can quote me a price for that painting?" Karen pointed to the canvas with the two figures.

Sarah gave her an odd look. "That's the one you want?" she asked.

"Yes."

"Why?"

"I am not really sure," Karen responded, pondering the question. "I think it's a combination of the colors and the movement…everything."

"I need to include it in the show," Sarah said, "But I can mark it sold. You didn't get my quote yet," she added.

"It doesn't matter," Karen went back to stand in front of the painting. "I want to buy it, and I know just where I will hang it."

"It's yours," Sarah said, turning away. "Where do you want to go for lunch?"

"How often do I come to Savannah?" Karen asked. "The Olde Pink House, of course."

Sarah made a face. "It's a tourist trap. We have some really good restaurants here now."

Karen shook her head. "I love the atmosphere, and I think the food is great. My mouth is already watering for the artichoke fritters."

"You're the guest," said Sarah. "Would you like to walk? It's just a couple of blocks."

"Definitely," Karen scooped up her purse and slung it over her shoulder while Sarah rummaged through her own bag for her keys.

Karen watched her friend secure the locks and bolt. "Is all that really necessary?" she asked as they descended the long, dark staircase.

"Oh yeah," Sarah said. This is a great area, but it can get rough, especially at night."

"Hard to believe during the day," Karen replied as they opened the outer door and stepped out onto the stone stoop. A pair of cement urns filled with drooping flowers adorned each corner. A massive oak formed an umbrella of shade in the front yard where a scrabble of grass fought for daylight.

Karen craned her neck and looked up at the building's

façade which was nearly covered by creeping ivy. A narrow balcony of wrought iron adorned the second and third floors. "Do you know the history of the house?" asked Karen.

"Not really. The old lady who owns it looks like she might have survived the Civil War. I'm sure she has a lot of stories, but she's a little off, if you know what I mean." Sarah tapped the side of her head and rolled her eyes. "Her son takes care of the rentals. I get the impression her family's just waiting for her to kick the bucket."

"That's sad," Karen was appalled. She couldn't imagine herself thinking of her parents in that way.

"The place is worth a fortune," Sarah continued. "I'm not sure what will happen to us renters if it goes up for sale." She hesitated, and then said, "I can barely afford it now since Tricia left."

Karen vaguely recalled that Sarah inherited a trust when her parents died, but she'd not had access to all of the funds. She also remembered Sarah's pain after the breakup with Tricia, her longtime partner. Following a bout of depression and self medicating, the artist buried herself in her work. Her upcoming exhibition was the fruit of that labor.

"Well, now you're going to be rich and famous so it won't matter." Karen assured her friend, while Sarah barked her short laugh. "And we'll all live happily ever after."

Turning the corner, they arrived at the Olde Pink House. They climbed the stone stairs worn smooth over time. Karen eyed a group in the foyer that was waiting to be seated. The gaudy shorts and rumpled t-shirts looked so out of place amidst the tasteful elegance. She smoothed the skirt of her lemon-colored sundress, wondering if she was the one who looked out of place. Sarah looked marvelous in a pearl-gray tank top and swingy black skirt that ended just above her knees.

Neither of the women had thought of reservations, but fortunately the lunch hour was winding down, and they had no trouble securing a table. The hostess asked if they had a preference, and Sarah smiled when Karen indicated the purple room upstairs.

They were seated beneath the portrait of a young woman with a cluster of black curls and a frank, dark eyed gaze. An ever-so-slight smile played about the woman's lips. Her gown looked like black velvet with embroidered scarlet sleeves and a white lace ruff circling the high neckline.

Across from them, above the fireplace, was one of the few paintings with a known subject: General James Oglethorpe. He had an arresting face with a significant nose and full lips.

"Geez," quipped Sarah, glancing at the paintings as she picked up her menu, "I'm not sure I like all those eyes looking over my shoulder while I eat. What is it you find so interesting?"

Karen squinted up at the lovely woman in the portrait. "The mystery I guess," she replied. "The woman appears to have such character, yet we don't know who she is. You know, all the paintings in the restaurant are authentic, but only three are identified. Oglethorpe there," she gestured at the painting, "And the original owner and his wife."

Sarah smiled. "Well, I know what an excellent judge of art you are."

Karen raised her empty wine glass. "I think we should order some wine and toast your success."

"Excellent idea. Only I need a real drink."

The waitress arrived at the table to take their order. The girl's dark hair was pulled back in a smooth bun and gleamed under the lights. Her skin was creamy and her eyes almond shaped and almost black. She spoke with a slight accent, Eastern European.

"I'll have a Gray Goose martini with a lemon twist," said Sarah.

Karen closed the wine list. "I'll have the same." She winked at her friend across the table.

The girl rattled off the specials in her charming accent, but they already knew their favorites and ordered a plate of artichoke fritters, two Caesar salads, pan seared sea scallops for Karen, and beef tenderloin au poivre for Sarah.

"Interesting," said Sarah, her eyes following the waitress. "If it weren't for the accent, I'd say she could be a distant relative of Sophia up there." She pointed to the painting above them.

"Sophia?" asked Karen.

"Well she had to have a name. I think it suits her. Kind of Italian."

Karen laughed. "We really are crazy."

Their drinks arrived promptly, and they clinked glasses. "To your continued success," saluted Karen.

"To our friendship," answered Sarah.

"Yes, always," Karen responded and took a sip. The martini was deliciously cold. It made her think of snowy fields. She wondered if the waitress was Russian.

"So, tell me what's new with you," Sarah asked, putting down her drink. "Are you writing?"

"Some," said Karen, setting down her glass. "I do an occasional column for a local paper and a lot of PR stuff for Mira's school. I substitute teach there too." She looked across at Sarah. "I know it must sound boring to you, but I'm satisfied with my life right now."

"Not at all," Sarah replied. "I envy you. So how's Ahab?" she added with a twitch of her lips.

Karen raised her eyebrows.

"Okay, okay, just kidding. Any guy who can father the sweetest child in the world can't be all bad."

Karen smiled. "Wait till you see her. Mira is so independent now, and horse crazy."

They paused as the salads were served, and enjoyed the crisp greens and crusty croutons before continuing the conversation.

"Sami is fine, I think," said Karen.

"You think?" Sarah echoed. She stared, her fork poised mid-air.

Karen looked down at her drink, her hand gently rubbing the base of the glass. "I wanted to talk to you about that," she began.

"Go ahead," Sarah encouraged. She broke off a chunk of warm bread and sat back in her chair.

"Actually, it's about an incident," Karen continued. "A few weeks ago I went to Sami's office to meet him for lunch. There was a young man there who was..." Karen searched for the word.

"Scary."

"He was incredibly rude. Looked at me like I was a bug or something. Sami tried to brush it off. Told me the man was a colleague's relative. I found out later that was a lie."

Sarah sipped her drink but said nothing, letting her friend continue.

"I told my Dad about it yesterday. He thinks I'm being paranoid. Maybe he's right, but I can't shake this bad feeling that something is very wrong."

"I usually trust my gut feeling." Sarah said. "Why do you think Sami would lie about this man?"

Karen set down her fork. "I think he may be afraid of him, or is involved with him in something he doesn't want to be in."

"Finish your drink before our entrees come," Sarah urged. "I'm having another." She gestured to the waitress.

Karen drained her glass. "Sami asked me to trust him. That's all he'll say."

When the Russian girl arrived at their table, with a second martini for Sarah, Karen ordered a glass of Cloudy Bay Sauvignon Blanc.

"As I recall, Sami works at Emory. Associating with scary looking people is not good."

"What should I do? Wait and see what happens?" asked Karen.

"You'll have to decide that. But my brother Joe is a feeb. He's not a field agent, but he would probably know someone you could talk to."

"I remember him. We met in Duck." Karen recalled a long ago weekend at the Outer Banks beach house with Sarah, Tricia, Sami and herself. Joe, a mild-mannered young man with the same red hair as his sister, had joined them at the end of the week.

"He's FBI? I thought he was a computer whiz or something."

"He is," said Sarah, "for the Bureau. He's a special agent but keeps a low profile. Lives in DC but uses the place in Duck whenever he can get away."

"He'll probably think I'm crazy, but it would make me feel better to talk to someone."

"Don't worry about it," said Sarah. "Joe's not like that. I'll call him tonight and get back to you tomorrow. Wait a minute…" she added, retrieving her purse. She pulled out a bulging appointment calendar and tore off a scrap of paper. She wrote the name: Joe Miles, and scribbled a phone number beneath it. "Here," she passed the paper to Karen. "But let me call him first."

Karen's appetite peaked when the plate of scallops with caramelized onions appeared in front of her. "You see, I told you the food was good," she said.

"Yeah, after two martinis everything tastes good." Sarah set her empty glass down and sniffed the succulent beef on her plate.

"You're not having another?" Karen widened her green eyes and stared at Sarah.

"Nope, two's my limit," Sarah responded. "Did I ever tell you my Tarzan martini joke?"

"I don't think so," Karen glanced around the room where several more patrons had been seated.

"Well, Tarzan comes swinging home on a vine to his tree house and says, 'Jane! Bring Tarzan martini.' He downs it in one gulp and says, 'Jane! Bring Tarzan 'nother martini.'" Sarah had lowered her voice and was mimicking a Tarzan-like scowl.

"He downs the second martini, and says, 'Jane! Bring Tarzan 'nother martini.'"

An elderly couple at the next table turned to stare at Sarah and Karen.

"And Jane says, 'Tarzan, what wrong? Tarzan never have more than two martinis.'"

"And Tarzan says, 'Jane, it's a fucking jungle out there!'"

Chapter Twenty Five

Washington, DC

Joe Miles flinched when his Blackberry rang. He was following a trail of evidence on an especially frustrating investigation, and he did not want to be disturbed. Reluctantly, he checked the caller ID and was surprised to see his sister's name.

Ever the night owl, she rarely called him during working hours. But then, it was 9:30 pm in DC, and most sane people were not working.

He clicked the receive button. "Hey sis, is this an emergency?"

"Well, hello to you too," Sarah responded.

"Sorry, sorry…I'm just bogged down in cyber hell with this case I'm working on. I can't seem to get a break."

"Jesus, you make it sound almost interesting."

Joe smiled, and rubbed his eyes. He resisted the urge to respond to her gibe. He never won with her.

"What are you doing working at this hour? Sarah asked. "Why aren't you out screwing some little feebie trainee?"

"The field agents have dibs on them," he responded. "Did you call to discuss our love lives?"

"Ooooh, you're so mean," she said, but he could hear the smile in her voice.

"Actually, I'm calling on business. I had lunch today with my roommate from Vanderbilt, Karen. Do you remember her?"

"Oh yeah! An absolute ten with incredible tits. Married

to the Arab guy, right?"

"Don't be a pig," Sarah said, then fought back the bicker voice she'd employed since childhood with her sibling.

"I had lunch with her today, and she is really scared. Her husband, the Arab, who happens to be quite a prominent doctor at Emory, is being visited by some unsavory people."

"So?" he countered.

"So, I told her I would call you and maybe you could put her in touch with an agent who investigates this type of thing," said Sarah.

"Oh Jesus, God, terrorists coming out of the woodwork," Joe looked back at the file on his desk and wondered how he could get out of this conversation.

"I know, but come on, you tell people to be vigilant and then blow them off when they take you at your word."

"Who is them?" he asked.

"You're the fucking FBI!" Sarah's composure was quickly disintegrating. "All I'm asking for is a name, someone who follows up on suspicious leads."

She took a long breath. "Listen Joe, Karen is not some bimbo. She is goddamned scared and she might have reason."

"Okay, calm down. I can check with someone here," he conceded.

"Can you get back to me tomorrow?" she asked.

"Yeah, I'll get you a name." he said.

"Thanks Joe, you always come through."

He almost laughed at that, but bit his tongue instead. "So, are you ready for the big exhibition?"

"Yeah, except I feel like puking every time I think of it," she quipped.

This time he did laugh. "Don't worry, I'll be there to hold a bucket for you."

"Very funny," she made a face, but then smiled. "I have a painting for you."

"Something dark and anguished, I hope."

"Actually, the opposite," she replied. "I think you'll be surprised."

"I'm looking forward to it."

"See you Joe, love you," she ended.

"You too kid. Ciao."

* * *

Joe pulled off his wire-rimmed glasses and ran a hand through his springy auburn hair. The hallways were dimly lit and silent. His cubicle was one of the few still occupied. Switching off his desk lamp, he sat back in his chair and thought about that summer at the beach. It had to be six or seven years ago, two years before his parents died.

He remembered Karen well, and she was a knockout. She was also intelligent, and possessed a directness he had encountered in few people. He'd liked Sami too. The man had a good sense of humor but also an earnestness that appealed to him. In his estimation, an undercurrent of paranoia regarding Islam did exist, but that didn't mean it was completely unfounded. Bad people are out to get us as we learned on September 11th.

Sarah was not one to give credence to bogeymen. She wouldn't have asked the favor unless she believed something might be wrong. He picked up his Blackberry and scrolled down his contacts list. He punched the button and walked over to a window that looked down on Pennsylvania Avenue. He watched the lights glimmering across the city.

"Hello," the voice was throaty and rich, a whiskey voice.

"Hi Lois, it's me, Joe. Am I interrupting anything?"

"Only a carton of leftover Chinese take-out. Is this a social call?"

"A little of both. Could I entice you to meet somewhere

for a bite of food or a drink? Hell, make it both."

The answering laugh was as delightful as her voice. "I'm intrigued. It will have to be someplace casual. I just got comfortable."

"You name it," he said.

"How about Clark's?"

"Want me to pick you up?"

Small hesitation. "No, I'll meet you there. Twenty minutes okay?"

"Sounds good. See ya." Joe tried to remember when he had last seen her. Certainly it was before she had joined the Counterterrorism Division. Slipping his Blackberry into his pocket, he returned to his desk. He clicked the logoff icon on his computer and gathered up his papers, locking them in a lower desk drawer. His eyes scanned the cubicle as he replaced his glasses. He was farsighted so only the lower portion had correction for reading, but he was used to wearing them. Pulling a gray suit jacket off the back of his chair, he slung it over his shoulder and headed down the empty corridor towards the elevator.

Joe lowered the windows of his silver Porsche as he pulled out of the parking garage. He had tossed his jacket on the seat beside him and was pulling off his tie. The muggy air washed over him as he breathed in deeply the scent of the city; warm sidewalks, car exhaust, exotic foods, trash, and crowds of sweating people. The night surrounding him was alive and pulsing as he drove down Pennsylvania Avenue. Plate glass windows reflected the lights and traffic, blocked in places by dark leafy trees. The stars were lost in the smog.

He turned right on 14th and then took another right at M Street. People thronged the streets in the heart of Georgetown; tourists, students, bureaucrats and foreign nationals. Like his sister, Joe was a night owl. When he spotted Clark's, he turned onto Wisconsin Avenue at the light. Pulling into the parking garage on his right, he pushed the oversized button and took a ticket from the machine. Parking in a corner spot next to the wall, Joe raised his windows before shutting off the engine. He glanced around the cavernous concrete room illuminated by bluish fluorescent lighting, while he yanked off his tie and threw it on top of his jacket. After locking the car, Joe headed for the elevator which would take him to the third floor of the mall where there was an entrance to the restaurant.

By the time he arrived, Joe had rolled up his shirt sleeves and hoped he looked casual enough in spite of his dress slacks. Clark's was as inviting as the parking deck had been inhospitable. Leather upholstered booths lined one wall with a long bar directly across from them. The lighting was soft and glowed from small lamps perched on the tables and Tiffany shades hanging above the bar. Joe scanned the room before taking a seat at the bar. He perused the menu before ordering a Newcastle on draft.

Resting his bare forearms on the bar, Joe wrapped his hands around the cool glass. It felt good. After briefly checking his image in the mirror, he let his eyes wander over the crowd. A blonde-haired woman several seats down from him smiled and turned to whisper something to her mousy-haired companion. He smiled and looked away. It had been a long while since he'd gone trolling. He was out of practice.

Lois and Joe spotted each other as soon as she entered the restaurant. Her generous mouth broke into a smile as her dark eyes took him in. "Long time no see," she drawled as he stood up to face her. She gave him a brief hug and a peck on the cheek. She smelled like soap and her short dark hair was damp and clung to her head as if she just emerged from a shower.

"You look good," said Joe, and he meant it. She wore faded jeans and a white v-necked T-shirt.

"Likewise," Lois pointed to his beer mug with its frost already ebbing away. "Got one of those for me?"

"You bet," he gestured to the bartender. "Do you mind sitting at the bar?" he asked.

"Not at all," she responded, easing onto a stool and cradling her leather satchel purse in her lap. Joe wondered if she was packing. Her dark eyes took in the room at a glance as she was trained to do. They came to rest on the blonde who was watching them in the mirror.

"Anyone you know?" she asked.

Joe smiled, "Not yet. What's your pleasure?"

The bartender materialized in front of them, wiped off the counter with a damp towel, and set two menus down. "If that's draft, I'll have the same," said Lois, pushing aside the menu.

"Not hungry?" Joe asked, "The invitation included dinner."

"I'm starved," she quipped, "And I'll have the cheeseburger with cheddar and fries."

Joe knew her training kept her fit, but he still marveled that her diminutive frame could pack away so many calories.

Lois seemed to read his mind, "No tofu and arugula for this girl."

"I remember," said Joe. The bartender set her beer down on a paper coaster, and Joe ordered burgers and fries for the two of them.

They clinked glasses. "To old times," said Lois, her eyes narrowed and dancing with mischief.

Honey. That's the word that came to Joe's mind as he looked at her. The smooth skin of her face and throat was golden like honey. Her voice was full, rich and sweet.

"You hinted at business," she said after taking a swallow of beer. She appreciated that it was just the right temperature, cool but not icy.

"Yes," Joe answered. "Why don't we eat first and then talk outside." Lois nodded and looked thoughtful. They caught up on each other's lives while they ate. Joe discovered he was ravenous and finished all of his burger and most of his fries. He offered Lois another beer, but she shook her head.

"Do you like your job?" he asked, watching her twirl a French fry in a dollop of catsup.

"Yes, I do," she answered. "I still have a lot to learn, but I think it's a good fit." She dropped the fry on her plate. "Does your business have something to do with my job?"

"It does, but I also wanted to see you."

"I'm glad you called," she replied. "I think I'm ready for some fresh air. What about you?" She stood up and slung her purse strap across her shoulder.

"Sounds good."

"Thanks for dinner," Lois added while he settled the tab.

"My pleasure," said Joe, leading the way towards the door. The room was now packed with patrons waiting for a place at the bar. Joe and Lois paused outside on the street. "Where are you parked?" he asked.

"The garage on Wisconsin," she answered.

He nodded. "I thought it would be nicer to walk outside instead of going through the mall. Lois fell in step alongside him, and Joe searched for a place to begin.

"My sister called me tonight from Savannah. She asked if I could give her the name of someone who works in the Counterterrorism Division."

Lois threw him a quick look but said nothing.

"A close friend of hers is married to an Arab doctor. He is a neurologist at Emory University Hospital. He also works closely with the CDC."

"And…" Lois prompted.

"His wife has noticed a change in him since a visit two weeks ago by an unsavory looking gentleman of Middle Eastern descent. He refuses to speak with her about it."

"That's pretty vague," Lois said slowly. "Do you know the woman?"

"I met her a few times," Joe responded. "She and her husband came to our place in Duck one summer. I think he was interning at the time. They're both intelligent and didn't strike me as the paranoid type."

"Is he a Muslim?" she asked.

"I'm not positive, but I think so. The subject never came up." They had reached the elevator at the parking ramp. "I'm on four," said Joe. "Ride up with me and I'll take you to your car."

"Sure." As the elevator doors slid shut, Lois opened her purse and dug out a small white card which she handed to Joe. "Have her call me. As you know, the majority of leads I track down are from crackpots, but we can't take a chance."

The parking deck was not nearly as dismal with Lois walking beside him. Her eyes widened when the silver Porsche, crouching in the corner, flashed its lights at their approach. "Very nice," she said, running an index finger along the gleaming bumper. "You get a promotion?"

Joe just smiled and shook his head as he scooped up his jacket and tie and tossed them in the back seat. He held the door for Lois and enjoyed watching her ease into the low passenger seat.

"Where are you parked?" he asked sliding in next to her.

"The next floor up," she said as he cranked the engine. He lowered the windows and glanced at the rearview mirror before backing out. She watched his hand on the gearshift. The unnatural lighting shone through the window and glinted off the fuzz of wiry auburn hairs on his forearm.

As they rounded the corner going up the ramp, he spotted the candy apple red vintage Mustang. "You still have it," he said with an approving glance. "It looks great."

"Yeah, it's my baby." Her eyes traced the classic lines

with pride. "Well, thanks again Joe," she said opening the car door. She didn't give him a chance to touch her.

"Thank *you*," he answered with a crooked smile.

Lois paused before leaning in the open passenger window. "By the way, what is your friend's name?"

"Karen Nasser," he replied and reached over to clasp one slender hand. "Let's keep in touch."

"I'd like that," Lois gave his hand a squeeze, then turned away and headed for her car. "Hell of a body," thought Joe as he watched her walk away.

Chapter Twenty Six

Lois slid into the bucket seat of her 1972 convertible pony car. The bureau provided a dark, non-descript Ford which she drove most of the time. She saved the Mustang for special occasions. It had been a present from her brothers on her graduation from the Academy. She had grown up trailing her brothers, assisting them as they restored old cars. Tony especially was a classic car fanatic. By fourteen, Lois could dismantle and rebuild a carburetor.

Both brothers were cops like their father. She always thought of them when she turned the ignition key and revved the engine of her beloved Mustang.

Smiling as she eased out of the parking space, Lois recalled her family's reaction the Sunday afternoon she announced at the dinner table that she planned to be an FBI agent. Her father's meatball laden fork poised mid-air. Her brothers and their wives just stared at her. Even her nine-month old nephew stopped banging his spoon on the highchair tray and regarded his elders with trepidation at the sudden quiet.

"I know what you're going to say Pop," said Lois, putting up her hand. She'd learned long ago that attack is always better than defense. "I just want you to hear me out." She took a deep breath.

"You know I wanted to be a cop, like you and Mike and Tony. And you were against it, so I went to college like you wanted. And I graduated top of my class. But my dream hasn't changed. I still want to be in law enforcement. I know I'll be good at it." She looked around the table and then lowered her eyes. "And they want me," she added.

"You've been accepted?" her father, Frank, raised his bushy black eyebrows. "You applied without telling us?"

She was familiar with that look on her father's face. He had used it on enough of her boyfriends over the years. It was a miracle she ever lost her virginity.

"I wasn't sure they would accept me," she said simply. "I want this so much!" her dark eyes burned as she looked directly at her father.

"Not accept you?" her brother Tony broke in. "What, are they nuts? I bet you have more brains and guts than half the friggin bureau."

Frank glanced at his wife, who remained silent but had a little smile playing around her lips. "Well," he said, carefully wiping his mouth with his napkin. "I can't stop you, as you well know. It's a free country."

"I know that Pop, but I need you to understand. I want you to be proud of me."

"What the hell is this?" he said, throwing down his napkin. "You're my daughter. I'm always proud of you."

He stood up and gestured towards his oldest son. "Mikey, fill your glass and pass down the bottle of wine. We'll drink a toast to your sister."

The table erupted in noisy relief, everyone talking at once, Mama jumping up to fetch another bottle of red, and baby Niko resuming his banging with a toothless grin.

And that marked the beginning of her career, her introduction to the Academy and to Joe.

Despite an immediate physical attraction, they had little in common beside a will to excel. Both were aware of an unspoken competition. He was a faster runner, she was a better marksman. He nodded to her and smiled one day after she'd nailed her target five shots in a row. Lois nodded back, annoyed by the flush of pleasure that rose to her face.

A week later, following a grueling afternoon in Hogan's Alley, she saw Joe sitting on the steps of a townhouse used for training. A streetlamp haloed his auburn hair. It was early April but still cold. His breath blew little puffs of steam in the chill air of an early blue dusk. He smiled and rose when he saw her.

"How about a drink to celebrate the weekend?" he asked.

Lois hesitated. "We don't really know each other," she said slowly.

"Sure we do," he quipped. "We've been together all semester. But I'd like to know you better, Lois Castellari."

"Okay, Joe Miles," she said, treating him with a rare smile.

"Do you mind walking to my car?" he asked.

"Not at all," she replied. "I hope you drive better than you shoot."

And that was how it began.

Chapter Twenty Seven

Suburb of Washington, DC

Pulling into the small garage at the back of her townhouse, Lois did an automatic survey of her surroundings before exiting the car. She pulled the small .38 handgun from her bag and slipped it into her jacket pocket. The yard was dark but lights shone from windows in the unit beside her and threw humped shadows from the shrubs that separated her small patch of ground. Her neighbors were Chad, a cosmetic dentist, and his partner, Palmer, a fashion buyer.

The pair had formed a welcoming committee when she first moved into the townhouse. They presented her with a bouquet of puffy blue hydrangeas and a bottle of white wine. "Welcome to the gayborhood!" they joked. "We're your new gaybors."

Lois felt a twinge of guilt as she glanced over at their side of the yard and glimpsed the white roses climbing along the back fence. Lush hydrangea bushes drooped in front of them and periwinkles clustered in front of these. A plethora of herbs nestled between the flowers and she caught whiffs of rosemary, basil, and oregano.

Chad and Palmer had told her on numerous occasions to help herself to flowers or herbs whenever she liked. It was tempting, but when did she have time to cook? And the flowers always wilted and died when she forgot to add water.

Her own little nightlight flickered cheerily from the kitchen window. Lois opened the door and punched in the alarm code. She grew up in a tough neighborhood in Baltimore.

But she didn't remember people being afraid all the time, like
they were today.

Home sweet home. It wasn't fancy or even eclectic.
The battered chrome kitchen set was inherited from her
grandmother, as was the incomplete set of apple pattern
Franciscan earthenware. She had eaten many an authentic
Sicilian dinner on those dishes, and couldn't part with them
despite the chips. The room was small but cozy with her things,
tacky as they might be.

Lois slipped the gun back into her bag after checking
the safety and dropped it on a narrow wooden table along with
her car keys. Taking one more look out the window above the
sink, she closed the blinds. Humming, she selected her favorite
mug from a shelf and began to fill the teakettle from the sink.
Then she paused in her nightly ritual of making tea. The house
was still warm, despite the air conditioning cranked up to max.

Pulling open the refrigerator door, she peered inside.
Cardboard cartons with her discarded Chinese dinner
dominated the center shelf. A few bottles of condiments (God
knows how old) jumbled along the top shelf along with milk
for her coffee. At least that was fresh. "Pathetic," she mumbled,
inspecting the lower shelf on the door. She smiled as she
retrieved the lone bottle of Chardonnay. She dug around in a
drawer for an opener before noticing the bottle had a twist top.
How convenient!

Grabbing a wine glass from the rack, Lois looked around
for an ice bucket. The empty flour canister would do. Scooping
a few handfuls of ice, she scattered them around the bottle.
With her bag slung back on her shoulder, the chilled canister
cradled in the crook of her arm, and the wine glass in her hand,
she slipped out of the kitchen and down the narrow hall to the
combination living/dining room. Pausing there, she eyed the
papers she had planned to review which were spread across the
round oak dining table.

"Tomorrow morning after my run," she thought, and headed up the stairs to her bedroom. Her mind was too full to concentrate. Setting down the canister and glass, she plopped her bag on the table beside her bed and switched on the lamp. It bathed the room in a soft golden glow. Lois twisted the cap off the tall green bottle. After pouring a glass, she set the wine bottle back in the canister of melting ice. She carried it into the bathroom where she stripped off her clammy t-shirt and shimmied out of her jeans.

Turning the taps on the old-claw footed tub, she threw in a handful of bath salts and checked the water temperature. Warm but not hot. Back in the bedroom, she thumbed through her CDs and selected *Barge Burns...Slide Flies* by Dave Bargeron. She hadn't listened to the album since she'd last seen Joe. Slipping the disc in the machine she punched "play."

The melancholy notes of "Holly's Song" filled the room as Lois peeled off her bra and panties. She stretched and ran her fingers through her hair before returning to the bath. Flipping a switch for the ceiling fan, she retrieved a book of matches and lit a cluster of white candles that filled a shelf above the radiator across from her. She picked up her wineglass and eased into the warm scented water. Closing her eyes she pictured the gleaming brass of the trombone and the slow rhythmic slide.

The image was replaced by a lean, compact body hovering over hers. She blocked out the face, but recalled every detail of his body. He lowered himself slowly, keeping his weight on his arms and knees. Excruciatingly slow, until his chest hairs just grazed her nipples. He laughed when she strained upward, tightening his hands on her wrists. His kiss just skimmed her lips before descending to her chin and neck, his tongue exploring.

Taking a sip of wine, Lois rolled it around in her mouth before swallowing. It was crisp, cold and delicious. She let her hand skim down across her throat and come to rest on her left breast. The nipple under her fingers was firm. She groaned softly and set down her glass of wine. Her other hand slid down into the soapy water.

She opened her eyes when he paused and released her hands. His fingers traced down her body and spread her legs, trailed across her thighs, and lingered on the taut muscle. His expression was quizzical as he studied her, as if he were seeing a woman for the first time. She opened herself further, seeking to draw him in.

Lying back in the tub, Lois allowed the exquisite sensations and the music to wash over her. Through half-closed eyes, she watched the flickering candle flames dance in the breeze from the overhead fan.

"Joe..."

Chapter Twenty Eight

Washington, DC

Joe scooped his jacket and tie from the backseat of his Porsche and slung them over his shoulder. A hint of Lois's shampoo and soap scent still hung in the air. He locked the car and took the steps from the underground parking garage to the lobby of his condo building. His footsteps echoed on the stone floor as he crossed to the bank of mailboxes on the far wall.

He opened his box and retrieved a small stack of envelopes before heading to the elevator. After punching the button, he glanced around the lobby. It was empty, tastefully decorated and impersonal. The metallic doors slid open, and Joe stepped inside and selected 14 for his floor.

Leafing through his mail, he noted only one bill and the rest was junk. Fortunately he paid the majority of his bills online. The chime dinged, and the doors opened again.

Art deco sconces lit the way down the hall. He stopped at the last door and inserted his key in the lock. Closing the door behind him, he flipped the bolt in place and tossed his keys into the "catch-all" bowl on the table in the entrance hall. He dropped the pile of envelopes next to it. Across the room, the small bar was backlit by corner windows. He pulled off his glasses and dropped them on his desk as he walked to the bar. Scooping a handful of ice from the machine, he dumped it into a crystal tumbler and poured himself a healthy dollop of Makers Mark.

Joe took a sip of his bourbon and looked down on Dupont Circle, teeming with a pre-weekend crowd. It looked like a Reggae band playing. He could see the brass and drums but only caught a faint hint of sound through the insulated glass. Above the park, the lights of the city formed a jeweled mosaic against the black sky. "Such a beautiful illusion," he thought, taking another sip. He knew all too well what happened on the streets beneath that sky. He wished to be down in the park, dancing, happy, and oblivious, even if it couldn't last.

He thought of Sarah. He ought to send her an email with the information. Tracing the steps back to his desk, Joe dropped into his chair and switched on his computer. While it booted up, he kicked off his shoes and pulled off his socks. That felt good. His iPod sat in the docking station and he hit the "Play" button, not sure what he would hear. *In a Sentimental Mood* poured out of the speakers. Ellington and Coltrane...ah yes.

He scanned his inbox first, coupons from Barnes and Noble, a bank statement, an advertisement for Viagra which made him smile. How did that make it through his filter? He glanced at the Omega watch on his wrist. Late, but he knew his sister was seldom in bed before the wee hours. He wanted to hear a voice.

After punching in the number, Joe put the phone on speaker, and settled back in his chair, propping his feet on the desk. Sarah picked up after three rings.

"Well that was fast," she answered. "Isn't it a little late for you?"

"Come on, you never sleep. Do you want the name or not?"

"Shoot," she replied.

"Her name is Lois Castellari. She's with the Counterterrorism Division." He rattled off a phone number.

"Is she good?"

"She's better than good. She's smart and tough and the best marksman I've seen."

"Well, let's hope we won't need that," said Sarah. "The

name sounds familiar. Isn't that the chick you were so crazy about at the Academy?"

"Excuse me?" he began.

"Oh give it up, bro. You talked about her all the time, and you were walking on air. Who did you think you were fooling?"

Joe had no response.

"You never told me what happened," Sarah added.

"Nothing to tell. I was an analyst, she went into the field and was transferred to California. End of story."

"But she's back in DC now, right? Did you have a date?"

"It wasn't a date. We met for beer and a burger." Joe reached for his drink.

"Whatever you say," Sarah replied. "Listen, I've been thinking. You're probably right that this thing with Karen is overblown. But I know she'll feel better after talking to a professional. She was there for me during the "deadly dark days", and I need to be there for her."

"Sis..."

"You don't have to say it Joe. I knew you were there for me too. You always have been, since we were kids."

"One for all and all for one," he joked.

"Isn't that the three Musketeers? What happened to the third guy?"

"Fuck him."

"Are you shit-faced?"

"Not yet," Joe replied, contemplating his drink.

"Listen, you need to get your ass to bed. You're not cut out to be a drunk. Take it from me."

"Don't worry, I know my limit," he said.

"I'll bet," she quipped. "Have I ever told you my Tarzan Martini joke?"

Joe groaned. "You heard it from me."

"Really? I don't remember that."

"Goodnight Sarah."

"Goodnight Joe," she paused. "I love you."

"Ditto," he said.

Joe swirled the ice in his glass. He thought about pouring another but decided it was too much effort. The screen on his computer had lapsed into sleep mode and was black. The only light came from the windows across from him and bathed the room in an intimate glow. He thought how nice it would be to have a cigarette, which was really weird because he had never smoked except for an occasional joint in college. It just seemed like a cool thing to do while he sipped his bourbon, listened to Coltrane, and thought about Lois.

* * *

It was early summer when Joe first brought Lois to his parent's beach house in Duck, on the Outer Banks of North Carolina. They had taken great pains to keep apart at the academy hoping to squelch any rumors. Fortunately, their grueling physical routine and daunting work load left little time for leisure. They had one month to go before graduation.

The weekend off had hung like a mirage over the desert. Joe had created a CD mix of his favorite jazz and blues musicians and was pleased by Lois's enthusiasm. She'd never been to the Outer Banks, and he enjoyed pointing out the vertical clapboard beach homes and Jennette's Pier in Nags Head, the Wright Brothers Memorial in Kill Devil Hills, and finally the charming village of Duck. They stopped at a grocery store and packed up on food staples for meals, beer, and wine.

"I'm going to cook you a real Italian dinner," Lois crowed as she picked through garlic bulbs and onions. "Everything fresh, that's the secret," she continued, waving a bunch of oregano under his nose."

"I'm salivating already," Joe replied sniffing the

aromatic herb. I'll get the French bread. There's a little wine shop up ahead where we can get a good Chianti."

"Oh, Mr. wine snob. When have you ever had a bad bottle of Chianti?"

"Well you've got me there, but I've had plenty of bad Chardonnays, and we'll get some of that too."

"You're the host," she said with a devilish smile. "I'm at your mercy."

That nearly caused him to lose it. He ignored the twinge in his pants and answered with a jest. "Does that mean you left your gun behind?"

"Maybe," she said pinching a ripe tomato. "But I certainly hope you brought yours."

That did it. Joe really needed to get to the beach house, screw the fancy wine.

At the checkout counter, Lois joked with the clerk who by some miracle spoke Italian. Joe noticed the admiring glances she won from other patrons as she helped Joe load the conveyer belt.

Muscles rippled in her lean arms and her waist looked impossibly small as she twisted to pull a six pack from the buggy. A sky blue tank top set off her golden skin and her jeans left little to the imagination. As he handed over his credit card, Joe imagined encircling that waist with his hands and slowly peeling off those tight little britches.

* * *

On the short drive to the beach house, they talked and laughed, but Joe was on autopilot. He'd glance over to catch her smile, or admire the wind rippling through her close-cropped black hair. He'd never realized how erotic short hair could be on a woman. It formed to her head accentuating her gamin features making her look like an ethnic Tinker Bell. Joe laughed at the image.

"What?" she asked, narrowing her eyes.

Joe waved his hand. "I'm just happy to be here with you, and away from the omniscient bureau." He knew if he shared his thoughts she would slap him, and that aroused him further.

At last! Norwood Drive. Joe swung right and drove the short distance to the majestic Atlantic Ocean shimmering before them.

The Moon reigned high in the sky when they finally repaired to the kitchen and settled on grilled steaks, green salad with blue cheese, and a bottle of Chardonnay. They left dishes soaking in the sink and took their wine glasses out to the back porch. The pool below the deck was dimly lit. Its aquamarine hue was a stark contrast to the black ocean beyond.

Lois raised her glass and looked through it at the moon, fractured into segments of gold.

"What are you thinking?" asked Joe.

"I'm not sure," she replied. "I guess I'm a little intimidated. You own this?"

"Not me," he answered, "my parents."

Lois squinted at him through the dark. "Miles. Senator Gerald Miles? Is that your father?"

Joe sighed. "Yes."

"Holy shit!" Lois said, setting down her glass.

Joe came out of his chair and knelt beside her. "I am not my father," he said taking her hand. "Don't judge me by this." He gestured to encompass the house and the view. "Tonight I am Joe Miles and you are Lois Castellari. Nothing more."

"All right Joe Miles." Lois stood up and pulled her oversized sweatshirt over her head to reveal the body of a goddess bathed in moonlight.

"I think I'd like a swim," she said, glancing back over her shoulder at Joe before sprinting down the wooden steps and diving into the pool.

"God! Its cold!" she screamed as Joe did a cannonball and crashed in beside her.

"I'll warm you," he said pulling her close and searching for her lips. He eased her over to the steps where he sat and lifted her up to straddle him. She held his face between her hands and they kissed. Then she eased off his lap and ducked down beneath the water.

"Oh God!" moaned Joe. "Oh God!"

* * *

Joe stood at the window and watched the sun breaking the horizon. He'd opened the window so the sound of the surf rolled through the bedroom. Lois turned over in the rumpled bed and blinked at him.

"Is this a dream?" she asked.

Joe smiled, "I'm not sure," he answered. Returning to the bed, he snuggled against her, burying his face in her hair.

"Are you happy?" he murmured.

He felt her body stiffen. "This is beautiful," she said. "But...but, it's not me. I grew up in a duplex in Baltimore. This is, well, it's a dream."

"Then don't spoil it," he responded, taking her shoulders in his hands and bending down to kiss her eyelids.

When he arose from the bed, Joe stretched and announced that he needed a shower. "Do you need to pee first?" he asked. "Or, you could join me in the shower and pee.

Lois sat upright in bed, "You pee in the shower?"

"Of course," he quipped and closed the bathroom door behind him. A few seconds later he cracked it open and saw Lois still sitting up in bed. Her mouth hung open, but for the first time was not issuing a smart-ass retort. He slammed the door shut just before a well aimed pillow thumped against it.

Chapter Twenty Nine

Bull Island, SC

Mira perched next to Nate in the front seat of the jeep. Enthralled by his undivided attention and knowledge of Bull Island, she assaulted him with a steady stream of questions.

Karen slipped her cell phone out and checked again for messages. Scrolling down to Sarah's number, she figured she'd try one more time. Four rings and a transfer to voice mail. Just like the other times.

When driving away from Sarah's the previous day, she had noticed a black sedan parked down the block across the street. There were two people inside, but Karen was too far away to see any details. She and Sarah had passed the same car on their walk to the restaurant. At the time it struck her as odd. Her mind told her she was being foolish, but she couldn't shake the nagging doubt that it had something to do with her.

"Who do you keep calling Mommy?" asked Mira, twisting around in her seat to observe her mother. Karen flipped the cell phone shut and stuffed it back in her pocket.

"Just Sarah, sweetie, she promised to call me today, and I can't seem to get hold of her."

"Why don't you leave a message?" suggested the little girl, her interest aroused. "Is it something important?"

Karen smiled and shook her head. Nate's eyes met hers in the rearview mirror, and he returned her smile. "Would you like to see the Boneyard Beach before we go back?" he asked the little girl. Impressed by his perception, Karen voiced her approval of the plan.

Mira was not so easily distracted. "Maybe she is painting a picture for her show. I don't like to stop when I'm making something."

The logic of her daughter's simple answer surprised Karen. "You are probably right," she answered. "Let's go to Boneyard Beach and look for old bones."

This time Mira took the bait and swiveled back to Nate. "Why do they call it Boneyard Beach?"

"I'm going to show it to you first," he replied with a wink. "And then you can tell me." Mira crowed with delight at the irresistible challenge.

Nate veered off the road and followed a bumpy track for a while. At the end, he parked the jeep and told them they would have to walk the rest of the way. "Don't worry, it's not far," he assured them. After spritzing their exposed body parts with bug spray, they set out along a narrow path. Quickly swallowed up in green forest, only the cawing of birds and the whine of mosquitoes broke the silence.

A distant whooshing pricked their ears and grew quickly in volume; the unmistakable sound of waves crashing on the shore. The forest ended abruptly, and the three stopped and stared at the surreal landscape in front of them. Mira was speechless for once. She glanced up at Nate, her dark eyes wide with wonder.

Hundreds of dead bleached trees lay strewn across the beach, with some hunkered down in the shallow waters. They shimmered in the glow of late morning sunlight, stark white limbs arching over the sand like the skeletons of giant mystical beasts.

"Dragon bones," Mira whispered. Then with a whoop, she charged forward across the sand.

Karen remained still. The crashing surf and golden light transported her back in time to some prehistoric place that was as ominous as it was beautiful. She watched her daughter cavorting among the skeletons.

Finally she spoke. "I forgot my camera but nothing could capture this." Nate nodded, and then with Karen, followed in Mira's wake across the shell strewn beach. At the water's edge, Karen pulled off her sandals and let her toes curl in the cool hard-packed sand.

Nate and Karen fell easily in step, while Mira scampered ahead like a sprite, pausing sporadically to inspect a shell or some other sea treasure.

"Careful of the water," Nate cautioned the little girl. "The rip tides are pretty strong here." She turned back and waved her acknowledgment.

"My dad's taught her all about them," said Karen. "He's making her a regular islander." She brushed back strands of hair the wind had pried loose from her pony tail and whipped across her face. "Has he been to this beach with you?"

"Oh yes, he fishes here all the time," Nate replied.

He smiled and tiny lines crinkled around his astonishing eyes. She realized the slight overlap of his front tooth was probably an asset after all.

"My husband would love this place," she said.

"Does he fish?" asked Nate.

"God no!" she laughed recalling an image of Sami bobbing in a john boat on the sound alongside her father. His face had been a mask of misery beneath the floppy hat while John, blissfully unaware, was describing bait.

"He's more of a golfer, like my mother. He's also a reader and very much a romantic. His mother was a history teacher at Birzeit University and also a phenomenal story teller. Sami has the same talent. I think Mira will too. They are actually very much alike."

"You should bring him here. This place was made for stories."

"Yes," she agreed, they could weave a magic carpet out

of this. "My father said you've written books. What are they about?" She looked up at him and he sensed she was genuinely interested, not just making conversation as most people did.

"About the islands, the people. I grew up here." He had retrieved a twisted branch of driftwood and was running his hand along the smooth silvery surface. "Everything is changing so fast," he continued, looking out over the water. Karen nodded but remained silent.

"I'm not a Luddite," he gave her a sideways glance and a rueful smile. "Change is inevitable. But the Gullahs have a unique culture, stories and beliefs that stretch back to Africa. It would be sad for that to be lost."

He stretched out his hand holding the branch to encompass the island. "This too," he added. "If we kill all the wild places, I believe something will die in us."

"I understand," said Karen, "And I'd love to read your books." She put up a hand to shade her eyes as she watched her daughter, crouched over a tidal pool.

"Growing up, I only spent the summers on Daufuskie, but it has always been my favorite place. A wonderful escape. I want Mira to have that."

Nate nodded and then saw Karen check her watch.

"Do you need to get back?" he asked.

"We probably should," she replied. "Mira definitely needs a nap after all this excitement. And I am expecting a call from my friend."

"Is she a local artist?" asked Nate.

"Yes, she actually grew up near Washington, DC but fell in love with Savannah. She's been here five or six years now. Her name is Sarah, Sarah Miles."

"I know of her," he answered. "She is very original."

Karen gave him an appraising glance. "You are a man of many interests," she said. "I can see why you and my father get along so well."

As they trudged back along the dirt track, Karen's cell rang. She fumbled it out of her pocket.

"Hello?"

"Hey there, it's me." Sarah's voice sounded far away. The reception was poor on some parts of the island.

"Sarah! I'm so glad to hear from you." Karen stopped and leaned back against the trunk of an ancient pine, swatting at a mosquito.

"What gives?" asked Sarah. "I got your umpteen messages. I was working. I never answer the phone when I'm working."

"That is so funny! It is exactly what Mira told me. She must be channeling you," said Karen.

Mira turned at the sound of her name and cocked her head as she watched her mother. Karen smiled at her and winked.

"Great minds think alike," Sarah quipped. "You sounded kind of stressed, is everything ok?"

"Yeah, fine." Karen began walking again and followed closely behind Nate and her daughter along the winding trail. "We just had a fabulous tour of Bull Island and are heading home now." Karen hesitated. "Do you have any news?"

"Yes, I talked to my brother and he got me a name," Sarah said, watching the black sedan parked across the street from her building. It was the same car she saw yesterday when they walked to the restaurant. Odd.

It had been sitting there for the past half hour or so. She'd first noticed it while she was cleaning brushes in her studio and happened to glance down to the street. She pulled the curtain aside to get a better look and saw a flicker of movement inside the car. In another minute, it started up and drove away.

"Listen, why don't you come over to Savannah tonight?" Sarah asked. "We could talk about this over dinner. You may recall what a lousy cook I am, but I know all the great take-out places."

"I'm not sure I ever tasted your cooking, but yes, I can do that." Karen answered. "What time?"

"Let's say sevenish?"

"Perfect. I'll check with my mom, but there shouldn't be a problem. If you don't hear from me, I'll see you at seven."

"See ya."

Sarah looked down at the name on the pad and circled it, Lois Castellari. They'd call her tonight. She looked back at the street, but it was empty.

Chapter Thirty

Daufuskie Island, SC

Mira was outraged at the prospect of a nap. "Why can't I come with you to see Aunt Sarah," she pouted, arms crossed tightly against her chest.

Karen put her arm around the little girl who was sitting beside her on the overstuffed floral couch. "I told you we are talking business tonight, and Papa wants to take you to Swampside Mary's. You need to go before Daddy gets here, you know how he feels about Ned."

Karen could see the conflict roiling in her daughter's eyes. "What if he doesn't come?" Mira asked.

"He'll come, I'm sure of it. And Aunt Sarah may come for a day. We can take her all over the Island. She said she'd like to go to the Silver Dew Pottery. Do you remember it?"

"Yes!" Mira piped, "I bought the pink starfish. When will she come?"

"I'll find out tonight," Karen said. "And now it's time for a little nap so you are ready for Papa tonight."

"Can I read a book first?" Mira asked, her expression was innocent, but Karen knew better.

Alice had come up behind her daughter and granddaughter and admired their two dark heads bent together. "How about if Nana reads you a book?" she asked, playfully tugging Mira's ponytail.

"Okay," the little girl jumped from the couch and crossed the room to retrieve her Disney Princess backpack from a corner. She pulled out a stack of books, spread them on the floor, and struggled over which one to pick. She finally snatched up Beauty and the Beast and hugged it to her chest. "Belle is my favorite princess," she announced solemnly to her grandmother.

"Mine too," agreed Alice as she shepherded the little girl up the stairs to the bedroom.

"Will you come with Papa and me to see Ned?" Mira asked.

Alice winced, "We'll see sweetie."

Karen grabbed a Diet Coke from the fridge and headed out to the screened-in porch. Flopping down in one of the comfortable chairs, she sipped her cold drink and scanned the pond for the resident alligator. A white egret circled and then landed on the opposite shore. Another soared across the water to join the first. Karen knew by early evening there would be at least a dozen or more basking in the last rays of the sun. She had always wondered what drew them to the same place. Like an expectant audience, they appeared to be waiting for something.

Her parents' chocolate lab had been sleeping on a hooked rug under the ceiling fan. She raised her head, got slowly to her feet, and ambled over to Karen. "Hey there Hershey girl." She caressed the dog's velvety ears and smiled into the soulful amber eyes. "Look at those whiskers. You're turning into a gray lady."

Her phone jangled for the second time that day.

She retrieved it from the glass end table and flipped it open, jabbing the receive button. "Hello?"

"Hi love, it's me," Sami's voice sounded hollow over the airwaves. He must be on his car speaker phone.

"Sami! Hi…"

"How is the vacation going? Are my best girls having fun?"

"Always," she smiled and gave him a rundown on their adventures, briefly describing the morning with Nate and Mira at the beach.

"Nate is a good friend of Dad's, and quite a hunk," she teased.

"Hmm, should I be worried?" asked Sami, his eyes scanning the horizon where thunder clouds loomed ahead. "Is he hunkier than me?"

Karen laughed. "No one is hunkier than you." She scratched the mosquito bite on her leg and narrowed her eyes when she spotted a suspicious trail in the water. Hershey made a low guttural sound and gave a few short woofs.

"Hey, I think I see Oscar," said Karen, standing up and crossing the porch. She made a whistling sound as the ten foot reptile glided past, bulging eyes and tail skimming the surface. "He's grown."

"Welcome to the jungle," quipped Sami, "I hope you have plenty of bug spray."

Karen ignored the remark. "When will you get here?" she asked.

"I got away early, and am heading your way as we speak. You were right, I needed a break."

"Sami that's great!" she responded.

"I should reach Hilton Head around seven or eight depending on traffic...and the weather," he added, frowning at a distant crack of lightning. He vividly recalled standing on the Clubhouse verandah at Haig Point and watching the retreat of a thunderstorm. A sudden boom shook the ground and a blinding flash exploded up a pine tree less than 20 yards away. Stunned, he watched as a huge crow dropped from the upper branches of the tree. He went later to inspect where the lighting had torn a jagged double path up the rough bark. The big black bird lay shiny and stiff in the wet grass.

His thoughts returned to his wife as she continued speaking. "I was just telling Mom I planned to take the ferry over and drive to Savannah to see Sarah. Why don't you meet us?"

"I almost forgot, she has an exhibition next week, doesn't she?" he asked.

"She does and she's pretty nervous." Karen thought about mentioning the strange car but decided it could wait. She would like to speak to Sarah's contact first.

"I'm not sure I'll be there in time for dinner," he answered. "Looks like I am heading into a storm, but I should make it in time for a nightcap. I'll call when I get close."

"That would be perfect. She's moved to a place in the historic district in an incredible old house." Karen read off the address. "Do you need to stop and write it down?"

"No," he said. "I can remember it."

She knew he could and wished her mind worked that way. "Hopefully we can make the 10:30 ferry back to Haig."

"It's a date," he said. "Love you."

"I love you too," she answered. "See you tonight."

Sami switched on his headlamps as he observed the stream of lights heading towards him on the opposite side of the road. He jabbed at the radio, but the static quickly annoyed him and he shut it off. "Damn rain!"

* * *

Alice had joined Karen on the porch and caught the tail end of the conversation. "Was that Sami?" she asked.

"Yes, he is driving now and should be here tonight. He's going to meet me at Sarah's."

Alice sat down across from her daughter. "Mira told me she thought you were worried about Sarah. Is anything wrong?" She reached down to scratch Hershey who was settling at her feet.

"No, I just couldn't get in touch with her. I was probably just being paranoid."

"Like your poor old mother," Alice quipped. "I know what you and your father say about me, and it may be true. But I also know when my daughter is unhappy, and I'd like to be trusted enough to help if I can."

"Oh Mom," Karen was taken aback by the hurt she read in her mother's eyes. She came over to Alice, sat next to her on the sofa and put an arm around her shoulders. "You always help Mom. It's just that I'm afraid I might be imagining things. I don't want to get you and Dad upset for no reason."

Alice took Karen's hand. "So smooth and lovely," she said, comparing it with her own. My hands were once like that. You will forever be my little girl, just like Mira will be yours. I won't pry if this is something between you and your husband, but don't lock me out to spare my feelings." She raised her head to look directly at Karen.

"I won't Mom. I promise. Sami will be here tonight. We'll talk after dinner and maybe tomorrow I'll have a better idea of how I feel. I love you Mom."

Alice smiled and patted her daughter's hand. "Likewise," she said. "You better get moving if you are going to clean up and make that ferry." Her voice had taken on its didactic tone and Karen was relieved. Her mother rarely displayed a chink in her armor, and Alice's vulnerability frightened her.

"Tell Sarah hello for us, and we look forward to her exhibition," Alice added as Karen hustled off to shower and change. She looked down at the lab who yawned and rolled over on her back for a belly scratch. "We're a couple of good old girls, aren't we Hershey?"

Chapter Thirty One

Karen brought up the rear end of the stragglers hustling to make the 5:30 ferry to the Embarkation Center on Hilton Head. Daniel greeted each passenger as they stepped or hopped from the gang plank onto the boat. A brilliant smile creased his dark face when he recognized Karen. "Mrs. Nasser, so good to see you," he said, holding out his hand to assist her. His white uniform was spotless and dazzling in the afternoon sun.

"You too Daniel," she returned his smile. "Looks like I almost missed the boat." He leaned towards her, and glanced around to be sure they were alone. "Don't tell anyone," he said *sotto voce*, "But your mama called and told us you were on your way. We wouldn't leave without you."

Karen smiled and shook her head. "Thanks Daniel."

Normally she would climb to the second level, where she could enjoy the wind in her hair and the spray on her face. But this afternoon the sky over Hilton Head was churning with billowing blue-gray clouds, so she entered the cabin instead.

A boat hand was making the rounds with a clipboard. She recalled the young man from last season. He was gangly and suntanned with a thatch of light hair.

"Just one today ma'am ?" he asked with a shy smile.

"Yes just one," she confirmed, as she signed the passenger list. "But hopefully there will be two coming back."

Karen perused The Island Packet for events and gossip. She scanned articles on local events and issues in the main section. Normally, she enjoyed reading the personals with details about weddings, anniversaries, and obituaries, but today she was distracted. Pushing aside the paper, she stared out the window at the landscape that was familiar but forever changing. Boats bobbed and skimmed across gunmetal gray water where sky and sea seemed to join. The first fat drops of rain peppered the glass portals and tumbled down the surface in uneven rivulets.

As the boat chugged into the dock, Karen slung her purse onto her shoulder. Stepping out of the cabin, she was greeted once again by Daniel who snapped open a large black umbrella and presented it to her with a flourish.

"Daniel, you are too kind," she said. "Are you working the rest of the night?"

"Yes, ma'am, I'll be on the last ferry."

"Sami should be with me on the way back. I know he'll be happy to see you."

Karen wound her way through the pine straw littered parking lot and angled the umbrella in a vain attempt to escape the slanting rain. Clicking the button on her key fob, the lights flashed at her as she approached. She maneuvered into the front seat and struggled with the cumbersome umbrella. Tossing it into the back, she then dumped her purse on the passenger seat next to her. Gathering up her damp hair, she wound it into a knot and secured it with a tortoiseshell clasp. "Very chic," she mumbled, glancing in the rearview mirror as she started the car.

* * *

By the time Karen reached the bridge to the mainland, the rain had ebbed to a misty drizzle, so she cracked her windows. The air was moist and pungent. The wetlands below her stretched to the horizon in a deceptively placid landscape. She knew that life slithered among the reeds and teemed beneath the water's surface. The rumbling thunder served as an eerie backdrop.

The remainder of the trip to Savannah was a trek through suburbia lined with strip malls and housing developments, attractive but unremarkable. Karen's brain switched to autopilot while she pondered an evening with two people she dearly loved. Sami and Sarah had not always liked each other, especially at first. Karen often felt she was being pulled apart between them. They had eventually come around though, and Sarah was her maid of honor at the wedding with Tricia as a bridesmaid.

Pushing away thoughts of Sarah and Tricia's breakup, she recalled instead a glorious summer weekend in Duck. Staying in a weathered two-story beach house owned by Sarah's family, Karen, Sami, Sarah and Tricia had combed the beaches, sailed in the sound, and climbed the famous lighthouses. By day, they explored the islands from Corolla to Ocracoke, following along the pristine national seashore. At night, they dragged coolers to the beach where they ate seafood, drank wine, and told outrageous stories.

Karen pictured each of them. Sami glowing by firelight, his smile dazzling in his tawny face. Sarah dancing around the fire like a native, her copper curls bouncing and wreathing her laughing face. Tricia clapping as she watches, the fire flickering in her pale eyes.

The scene melted away as Karen approached Savannah. She concentrated on traffic as she pulled off the bridge and negotiated the famous old squares. Her eyes were automatically drawn to favorite buildings, statues, and fountains as she passed.

She parked her car by the curb on the side of Sarah's house. The building looked even spookier in the rain with its upper level swallowed by ivy. It stood black against the roiling sky. The straggly tree in front was mournful and dripping. Rain speckled the cracked sidewalk, so Karen reluctantly retrieved her umbrella from the backseat. She peered up at the windows on the top floor where Sarah had her apartment. They were dark and reflected the gloom like empty eyes. "That's odd," she thought. "There should be light."

She dropped her umbrella on the porch and rang the bell. She rang it a second time before trying the door. It was open. The staircase was dark and stank of rot and mildew built up over decades. Karen put her hand on the clammy banister and hesitated. If this was a movie, the audience would be screaming, "Don't go up there." She shook her head. Don't be ridiculous. Climbing the three flights, she caught her breath at the top landing before pounding on the heavy oak door.

"Sarah," she called. "Sarah, it's me." She turned the doorknob. The door swung inward and something inside Karen shrank back, even as she stepped forward into the room.

Chapter Thirty Two

Washington, DC

Joe had just arrived home when his Blackberry rang. He didn't recognize the number. Probably some telemarketer, but one never knows, so he punched the receive button.

"Joe Miles? Oh God, oh God..."

"Who is this?" his heart skipped a beat.

"Sarah. She's dead...Oh my God, they killed her!"

"What? Who is this? What the fuck are you talking about?"

"It's Karen. I just left her apartment. Jesus God, there was blood..." she began, her voice trailing off in a long wail.

Joe pulled off his glasses and pinched the bridge of his nose. "Goddamn it!" he said, "Goddamn it! Where are you now?"

"I called 911. But I had to get away from there. I came back to Hilton Head. I was going to my parents house on Daufuskie." She paused and tried to get her voice under control. "But after what happened to Sarah, I'm afraid. My little girl is with them."

"Tell me what you saw," Joe said. "Just calm down and tell me what you saw."

Karen leaned back in the car seat and caught her breath. "Sarah was on the floor in her apartment...her throat cut...there was blood everywhere...on the walls...Oh Jesus...

"What else?" he asked.

"Her paintings," Karen sobbed. "They were slashed. All of them. Who would do that?"

Joe closed his eyes. *"I painted one for you. You'll be surprised."* From their conversation the night before, Sarah's words reverberated in his head and cut to his soul.

"Karen, where is your husband?" he asked.

"I was supposed to meet him in Savannah."

"Don't!"

"He can't be involved in this."

"Do you know that?" Joe demanded.

She did not respond.

"Do you know that?"

"I don't know anything," she whispered, "I don't know anything."

"Listen to me!" he said. "Karen, are you listening?"

"Yes," she replied.

"You need to get away from there. Do you remember how to get to my house in Duck?"

"Yes."

"All right, you need to leave now and head up I-95. Wait! Do you know if you were followed?"

"I don't think so. I've been watching and only one other car drove in the parking lot after me. It was a family."

"They could have used a tracking device. Your car may not be safe. Can you get another car to drive?"

Karen pictured the man she had met in Sami's office, the man with the hate-filled eyes. "Oh Christ," she muttered, reaching up to massage her forehead.

"Karen, you need to think!"

"I know," she said, "I know," and began rummaging through her purse. "I have a key to my father's car."

"That's good," Joe said. "Switch cars now, just make sure no one sees you. I'm contacting our people in Savannah. You just get up here."

"And Karen," he added, "Do not use your credit card or your cell phone."

"I have to call my parents," she argued.

Joe groaned, knowing he would lose this argument. "All right," he conceded, "one call. Make it short and do not tell them where you're going. Just tell them you're safe."

She nodded, and then responded, "Okay."

"After you talk to them don't make any other calls. And don't answer your phone unless it's me. Do you understand?"

"Yes," she croaked, biting her hand to keep from sobbing. "Yes."

Joe disconnected the call. "Sarah! Damn! Damn! Goddamn!" He searched down his Blackberry's address book for Lois's number.

Chapter Thirty Three

Hilton Head Island, SC

Karen's mind was still spinning as she sat in her car in the embarkation parking lot. She had only been able to make the trip by focusing on details; the green, red, and gold of traffic lights reflected in the wet pavement, the glittering lamplights, and hazy street signs.

Her only thought had been to get away. To get home to her parents. To escape this nightmare. The rain had stopped, but the sky was still dark in a premature night. Her earlier vision on the drive to Savannah came crashing in as she crossed back over the bridge. Sarah laughing and dancing. Karen pushed it back. She couldn't think about that. She had to be strong, to get help, to protect her family. When her cell rang, she swerved and then pulled her car back in line. The car behind had honked at her.

When Karen reached a stoplight, she retrieved the phone from her bag and checked for the name on the missed call menu. Sami. She had pictured him arriving at Sarah's and wondered if the police were there yet. Would he walk in and discover the horrible scene as she had done? Did he know the men who did this?

By the time Karen reached the embarkation center, she'd had time to sort through events. The dark sedan she'd noticed in Savannah, was it connected? If Sarah was murdered because of her, then she had been followed. She began to shake. They could still be following her. Karen had rifled through her purse for the card Sarah had given her with Joe's number.

She looked down at the card still lying in her lap and thought about Joe's instructions. She dropped her phone back in her purse...for the time being. Karen lowered her hand from her face and stared into the darkness. She had to think.

Chapter Thirty Four

Washington, DC

"My God Joe! What the hell?" Lois set down the towel she'd been using to wipe her face. Having just returned from her run she was sweating profusely. "Did Karen give you any details?" she continued.

"She was hysterical," said Joe. "Told me there was blood everywhere." Lois heard him take a deep breath. "And Sarah's paintings were slashed."

"Jesus," Lois whispered, picking up the towel and mopping her forehead again. "Where is Karen now?" she asked.

"She called 911, then panicked and left. She called me from Hilton Head, the embarkation center to Daufuskie Island where her parents live. She is afraid if she was followed, they might hurt her family. That's why she called me." Joe heard himself speaking, slow and calm, describing his conversation with Karen. He wondered how this could be happening.

"That's good," said Lois. "We need to get jurisdiction on this right away. If the police screw it up, we may never get these guys. Do you think the husband is involved?" she asked.

Joe thought about that. "My gut feel is no," he answered. "But even if he's a target, he's dangerous."

"I agree. Give me the address and I'll alert the Savannah office," Lois scrambled for a pen and scribbled the information onto a calendar hanging above her. She bit her lip.

"I just don't understand why they would target Sarah," said Joe.

"If it was terrorists, I would guess they are sending a

message. If they can get to Sarah, they can get to Karen. I'd interpret it as a warning that they mean business. We'll get them Joe, no matter who they are. I promise."

He remained silent.

"I'm so sorry. Do you want me to come over?"

"No," he said quickly. "I need you to pull the strings while I get to Duck and wait for Karen." He drew in another ragged breath. "But thanks."

"I'm calling now. Keep me updated. And Joe...be careful."

* * *

Lois speed dialed the Savannah office and identified herself. She tapped her fingers on the yellow Formica counter as she waited.

The voice on the other end was polite and impersonal. "Special Agent Sanchez."

"Special Agent Castellari. How are you Gabe?"

"Hey I'm good." Lois heard the smile in his voice. "Is this business or personal?" It was a deep voice with just the hint of an accent.

"A little of both. I was just notified of a homicide in Savannah. I believe it might be linked to Homeland Security. The cops have been called, but I'd like to get some of our guys involved ASAP."

"When, where and who?"

She rattled off the information. "A close friend of the victim asked for a number at the FBI. She is concerned about some of her husband's associations. He's an Arab American."

Gabe sat back in his chair and scanned the information he had scribbled in his notebook. "Where does the personal enter?" he asked, scanning the office to see who was available.

"Joe Miles is the victim's brother. He spoke with her

the night before she was murdered and gave her my name and number."

"Joe? Man, I'm sorry." Gabe was silent for a few moments. "We're going to need more background. Can you get Joe to send us an email with everything he knows? I'll need info from the guy's wife, too. Does anyone know where she is?"

"Yes," said Lois. "She is on her way to meet Joe at his place on the Outer Banks. I'm going to Norfolk and putting a team on alert in case it's needed."

"Good," Gabe replied, and hesitated. "Joe's still with the bureau isn't he?"

"Yes. He knows what to do."

"Do you know if his sister was the target or collateral damage?"

"At this point we don't know," said Lois. "But we suspect the second. He or they are real bastards. Slit her throat and slashed all her paintings."

Gabe gave a low whistle.

"Do you anticipate any jurisdiction problems?" asked Lois.

"Let me worry about that. I'll contact you as soon as we know something."

"Thanks Gabe. I have a hunch we've uncovered something very bad here."

Chapter Thirty Five

Savannah, GA

Mahmoud lit a cigarette. His hand shook as he struck the match. Abdullah made a sound of disgust and fumbled for the button to lower the windows. He knew he must be the only Arab who didn't smoke, and he cursed the filthy habit.

"What is wrong with you?" Abdullah demanded.

"We should get away from this place," Mahmoud replied looking down the block where Karen had recently parked her car. They had followed the tracking signal and were surprised when it led them back to the victim's building. "She will call the police," he added.

"So what?" said Abdullah. "This is better than we planned. She will see for herself what we can do, and she will tell her husband." He squinted at the building. "Who can blame us? There is no proof. Besides, Allah will protect us."

Mahmoud had heard the phrase all his life and seen little to confirm the belief. "It is dangerous to stay here," he said. "Someone may remember the car. We can follow her later if we need to." He glanced in the rearview mirror and anticipated the flashing lights. He would die a martyr if Allah willed it, but he feared languishing in a foreign jail like his comrades in Guantanamo. Better to die than to be caged. A siren wailed in the distance.

"You may be right," Abdullah conceded, starting the car. "But first throw out that disgusting thing so I can close the windows and turn on the air conditioning." Just a few minutes of the humid air washing over him had left him feeling sticky and dirty. Atlanta was bad enough, but this was unbearable.

Mahmoud flicked his cigarette into the gutter as Abdullah pulled away from the curb. Abdullah was a desert Arab, but Mahmoud had grown up near Beirut, and was familiar with the humidity and smells of a port city. He closed his eyes and thought about home.

But another picture intruded, and the scene of an hour ago played out in his head. It had been easier than expected to gain entrance to the apartment. From their car, Abdullah and he had watched the red-haired woman as she approached the big dark building. She was not as pretty as Karen. Her hair was short and spiky, her face pale and freckled. Red hair was bad luck.

Mahmoud scanned the street as the two men approached the woman's building. Rain had driven the pedestrians inside, a clear sign that Allah was with them.

Abdullah turned the door knob and found it locked as he had expected. Mahmoud found the small button and speaker beside the door. He pressed it and heard the short buzz.

Soon a woman's voice came from the speaker. "Who is it?"

"Delivery," answered Mahmoud.

The buzzer sounded again along with a click. Abdullah opened the door.

Alert for any sound, Mahmoud paused in the dank hall. All was quiet. Blood coursed through him and pounded in his temples as he ascended the stairs with Abdullah at his back. They didn't speak, but used hand gestures to communicate.

Mahmoud knocked on the heavy door while Abdullah waited in the stairwell. The sound echoed in the empty gloom. He could see the small eye in the center of the door darken as the red-haired woman inspected him. He felt her presence on the other side.

"I wasn't expecting a delivery. Who is it from?" the

woman asked.

Mahmoud flashed a boyish smile before squinting down at the package. "Ah, looks like Karen Nasser, ma'am." There was a long hesitation and Mahmoud was afraid she wouldn't open the door. As he began to turn away, he heard the bolt slide.

The woman was prettier close up, in spite of her hair. Her eyes were clear and gray as the storm clouds outside.

Sarah smiled, "You can set it there," she said gesturing to a table by the door. "I'll be right back. I left my purse in the other room."

She paused at the doorway of her studio and searched for the light switch. Storm clouds had obliterated the late afternoon sun. Her head swiveled around when she heard a step behind her.

Before she could scream, Mahmoud's beefy right hand clamped across her mouth, while his left arm circled her waist and jerked her back against him.

Sarah struggled, kicking at his shins with the heels of her bare feet and scratching at his arms in a vain attempt to break his grip. The feel of her writhing body against his own aroused him. Abdullah materialized beside them, the knife already glinting in his hand.

"Mahmoud pulled her head back until he could see her eyes reflected in a mirror on the opposite wall. They frantically searched his face as Abdullah's blade carved a thin red line across her neck, cutting the vocal chords so a gag was no longer necessary. The men stepped back quickly to avoid being spattered by the woman's blood, and her body slumped to the floor.

* * *

Mahmoud and Abdullah pulled into a parking lot

several blocks from the waterfront and looked for a place to eat. They discovered a small diner that advertised gyros. Sliding into a maroon plastic booth, they were relieved to see the place was not full. A skinny black kid brought menus and took their orders while a beefy bearded man worked in the kitchen behind a counter. He looked up briefly when the pair entered and then went back to his griddle. An odor of roasted meat, vinegar, and grease hung in the air.

The two men ordered and took turns visiting the restroom to wash. Both were aware it was time for prayer, but there was no appropriate place to make devotions. They had been warned to avoid mosques and not to pray in public which would draw attention.

The waiter slid two oval plastic plates mounded with food onto their table The bread was chewy, the meat lukewarm and congealed with fat, the fries greasy and over-salted. The two men ate in silence, washing down their food with hot tea.

A little bell tinkled when the door opened, and two young women entered the restaurant. They were chatting and laughing as they scraped out chairs at a table not far from the booth where the two Arabs sat.

Probably students, the girls wore low-slung jean shorts and pastel tank tops. One was chubby with frizzy dark hair pulled back from her round face. The other was pretty in a washed-out, bleached blonde way. Her small breasts strained against the thin fabric of her top as she reached back to sling her purse on the chair.

Each ordered a beer and a Greek salad, checked emails on their phones, and exchanged gossip about a gross boy named Jack. Abdullah kept his eyes on his plate but Mahmoud couldn't restrain himself from periodically glancing over at the girls. The blonde met his eyes once and smiled. The corners of his mouth twitched, and he quickly looked away.

"What are you doing?" Abdullah hissed under his

breath in Arabic. "We cannot pray so you pass your time flirting with infidel *sharmutas?*"

"We were told to behave normal, not to attract attention," Mahmoud replied, poking the remains of his French fries, licking the salt off his finger. This is how the Americans behave," he continued with his characteristic shrug. "I am only following orders so we succeed in our mission."

Abdullah watched him with narrowed eyes but was unable to think of a good retort. "*Emshe*, let's go," he said, pulling his wallet out of his pocket. "We should check on the wife."

Mahmoud nodded his agreement and rose, tossing down two dollar bills as a tip. Following Abdullah, he passed by the table where the two girls were now engrossed in their meal. The back of his hand brushed lightly against the blonde's hair as he passed, but he kept moving as she scooted her chair forward. He was aroused for the second time that day.

* * *

"She must not have waited for the police," said Abdullah. "Do you think that is strange?"

Mahmoud was slumped in the passenger seat, sullen, irritable, and needing a smoke. "How would I know," he grumbled, "Everything the infidels do is strange. She is going back to her family," he jabbed his finger at the tracking screen where her car was a flickering green dot. "She will tell them what she saw and then tell her husband. He will understand the message and he will not refuse us again, *Inshallah*."

"*Inshallah*," Abdullah parroted, stretching his lips in feral smile as he recalled the mayhem in the dark apartment.

Mahmoud settled himself and closed his eyes. He felt the tension drain from his body, even as his stomach rumbled from their unsavory meal. He pictured the blonde girl with hair spilling across her shoulders and tiny nipples poking against her knit top. He imagined how the hair would feel in his hands, as he ran his fingers through it, twisted and pulled it into a silken rope.

Then he was back in the dark room. He and Abdullah looked up from the pale, limp body sprawled on the scuffed wood floor and looked around the studio. Diffused light poured down from a skylight while rain hammered on the glass. Both men stared at the paintings, illuminated in the eerie glow. As devout Muslims, they believed all depictions of humans and animals to be forbidden and idolatrous.

"*Bismallah, ar-Rahman, ar-Rahim* (In the name of God, most Gracious, most Compassionate)," Abdullah murmured, the bloodied knife hanging forgotten in his hand.

Mahmoud felt the hairs rise on the back of his neck. Like faceless demons, human-like forms cavorted across the canvases. He paused in front of one painting where two creatures appeared to reach out and draw him into their swirling dance of evil.

"We were told to leave a message," said Abdullah. Raising his knife, he slashed the offending canvas, breaking the spell. He attacked each painting in a frenzy, gouging the images and exorcising the devils.

"*Allahu Akbar!*" he said, surveying the destruction.

"*Allahu Akbar,*" Mahmoud affirmed, closing his eyes to drive out the offending images that beckoned him to hell.

Chapter Thirty Six

Daufuskie Island, SC

John Cameron set down his cocktail and cursed when the cell phone vibrated in his pocket. He raised his brows when he saw the name on the display.

"Hi kiddo," he said.

Relief washed over Karen at the sound of those two words spoken in his deep voice. She fought back the tears that welled up in her eyes. "Oh Dad," she said.

"What's wrong?"

"Something terrible, Sarah's dead."

"My God!" John pulled himself out of the porch chair. "What happened? Are you all right?"

Carrying a glass of white wine, Alice came out the back door. She frowned as she caught the tail end of his conversation. "Who is it?" she asked, wondering if someone on the island had been hurt.

John held up his hand as he listened intently.

"I don't know what happened," continued Karen. "When I got to Sarah's house the door was unlocked. She never left her door unlocked. I found her on the floor in her studio, blood everywhere, her paintings were slashed..." Karen sobbed, and then covered her mouth.

"Good God," John repeated. "Where are you now?" He motioned to his wife to wait.

"I'm at the embarkation center. Dad, I need to borrow your car."

"What?" John was pacing now. "Karen, you need to

come home!" He saw his wife close her eyes as she set down her wine glass.

"I can't," said Karen. "I think I was followed to Sarah's place. The people who killed her may have a device on my car. I can't explain everything now, but I need a different car that can't be tracked."

"Karen this is insane," continued her father. "You need to come home and call the police."

"I called 911, and I spoke with Sarah's brother. He works for the FBI. He said he would have people in Savannah handle things." Karen looked around the dark parking lot. "I am driving up to meet him in Duck."

"I'll come with you," said John.

"No, Dad, please." You and Mom need to take care of Mira." Karen was massaging her temple now.

"Where is Sami?" asked John. Alice had approached and was trying to hear what her daughter was saying. Her green eyes were wide with fear.

"He was supposed to join us after dinner at Sarah's," Karen answered. "He tried to call me about half an hour ago."

John searched his memory trying to replay their earlier conversation about her concerns for her husband. "You don't think he is involved in this?" he asked.

"No, I couldn't ever believe that," she responded quickly. John closed his eyes in a silent thanksgiving.

"But Sami knows something. He asked me to trust him, but we need help. That's why I called Joe. Dad, I can't talk anymore. I am not supposed to use the phone. Please, just take care of Mira. Tell her I love her, and I'll call as soon as I get to Duck."

"You call us the minute you get there," John demanded, "Promise!"

"I promise," she said. "I'll leave my car in the parking lot with the key under the back seat mat. I love you Dad. And tell Mom I love her."

Tears glistened in John's eyes. He set down the phone and with trembling hands, removed his glasses. Ceiling fans hummed above him and the ritual cacophony of croaking frogs pierced the night. His wife reached out to touch his arm.

"Sit down Alice," he said quietly and eyed his glass of scotch where the ice had melted away.

Chapter Thirty Seven

Savannah, GA

Sami switched off his GPS. He knew Savannah well enough to find Sarah's place. He wondered why Karen hadn't called back. He'd left a message an hour ago. "Hi love, made it through the rain and traffic and should be there in an hour. Call me."

She probably left her phone in her purse during dinner. It made sense, but he was mildly annoyed. The flashing lights and crowd of people up ahead caught his attention.

"Now what?" he thought, easing his car over to the curb. He climbed out, stretched his cramped muscles, and enjoyed the balmy night now that the rain had stopped. The street ahead was blocked off so he walked the rest of the way.

Must have been a bad accident," he thought as he approached. But oddly, there was no accident scene, just an ambulance, several police cars, and a crowd of gaping bystanders.

Sami looked up at the street sign and his blood froze. Two women next to him were whispering and pointing to the house on the corner.

"What happened?" he demanded. The older, frowsy woman backed up at first and exchanged glances with her companion. Then her need to gossip overcame her suspicion.

"Someone was murdered," she said, widening her eyes for emphasis. She glanced around to see if anyone else was listening. "We heard it's an artist, a woman," she continued, leaning in and putting her hand to her mouth. "Someone said she was a lesbian."

"Was she alone?" Sami asked. The woman shrugged and gestured toward the building where the paramedics appeared carrying a stretcher out the front door. The body was swathed in a blanket, the face covered. A tall black policeman was shouting, "Step back!" as he herded people away from the ambulance.

"How many were there?" Sami asked.

"How many what?" the big cop asked, and then followed Sami's eyes to the stretcher. "One's all I heard," he growled. "Listen, this isn't a news conference, read about it in the papers tomorrow. Step back! All of you!"

Two young men on the edge of the crowd had been observing Sami's exchange with the officer. Both sported navy blue FBI windbreakers. They spoke a few words before breaking away and heading towards Sami.

Sami was reaching for his Blackberry and realized he had left it in the car. He turned to leave just as the dark jackets approached him.

"Excuse me sir, I'm Special Agent Cartwright with the FBI," he began, "and this is Agent Lugad." They both flipped out their badges. May I ask you a few questions?"

Sami scrutinized the photos which matched their visages. The agent who had spoken was tall with regular features and clipped brown hair. His expression was genial except for the eyes. This was not a man you would cross.

Sami nodded, watching as they pocketed their IDs.

"Do you live in the area?" asked Agent Cartwright.

"No, I'm only visiting. I was on my way to meet my wife for dinner."

"Why did you stop?"

"The street was blocked. I thought there might have been an accident. I'm a doctor."

Cartwright raised his eyebrows and glanced at his

partner. "And where are you travelling from, Doctor?"

"Atlanta," Sami answered. He felt sweat trickle down the side of his face, but fought the urge to wipe it away. Agent Lugad was watching him. He was shorter than Cartwright, compact and wiry. His coloring and features looked Middle Eastern.

"Warm night," said Cartwright, appearing fresh and cool despite the windbreaker. "May I see your identification please?"

Sami sighed pulling his wallet from his pocket. "May I ask what happened here and why I am being questioned?" he asked, proffering his driver's license.

Cartwright produced a small notebook where he scribbled down Sami's information. "There was a homicide," he responded, watching Sami's expression, "A local artist, very bad. It's our job to question everyone in the vicinity for leads."

Sami looked over at the ambulance where the paramedics were closing the doors. "That's terrible," he said. "I'm sorry I can't be of any help."

Cartwright flipped his notebook shut and said, "I appreciate your time Doctor." He looked over at Lugad who gave a slight shake of his head before turning back to scan the crowd. No luck.

Sami felt the men's eyes on his back as he forced himself to walk, not run, back along the slick pavement, away from the onlookers, the flashing lights and the big dark house.

"What do you think?" asked Cartwright as he watched Sami walk away.

Lugad took the notebook from his partner and glanced at the notes. "I'd like to have held him but we have no grounds. Some lady I interviewed said the victim was gay. Could be a right-wing nut case, or a jealous lover. We just don't have enough info."

"I know. We should be getting an update any time."

Cartwright grimaced. "God knows we don't want to be crucified for racial profiling."

Lugad flicked his dark eyes at his partner. "Don't worry. We've got his information. We can find him if we need to."

Chapter Thirty Eight

"Answer God damn it! Answer!" Sami punched the number again and this time the call went directly to her message. Karen had turned off her phone. He had no choice. Selecting the number for John Cameron he hit the send button.

"Sami!" John answered. "Where are you?"

"I'm in Savannah," Sami replied, I just left Sarah's. Is Karen with you?" He leaned back in his seat and rubbed his forehead, saying a silent prayer.

"No," said John but she called. "She's all right and Mira is here with us. What the hell is this about?" His anger crackled across the air waves.

"Thank God," Sami choked, his voice breaking, "Thank God." He paused a moment, composing himself before continuing. "I'm being blackmailed John, by some very bad people."

"For Christ's sake why didn't you get help?" John demanded, his voice rising. "A woman is dead. It could have been Karen."

"I reported it to my superior at Emory," Sami protested. "He told me they would handle it and like a fool I believed him." Sami pounded his fist on the steering wheel. "I don't know who to trust now." He thought of the two FBI agents. Should he have confided in them? Why would they believe him? He couldn't take a chance on being held. His only thought was to get to Karen.

John nodded, "I probably would have done the same.

Who could anticipate such evil?"

"Where is Karen?" Sami asked.

"She is going for help," John replied, still stunned by Sami's revelation. "She wouldn't come home, and she refused to let me go with her. She was advised not to give her location or use her phone."

"Advised by who?" Sami asked, dread washing over him. Silence.

"John you know me. You know I would die for Karen or Mira. You've got to let me help her!"

John was watching his wife's lovely face, haggard from the strain. He saw a tear slide down her cheek as she nodded her approval.

"She is going to Sarah's brother in Duck," John said. "He's with the FBI."

"Joe Miles, I never thought of him," said Sami. The image of a summer past and a lean red-haired man flashed through his mind. "That must be why Karen went to see Sarah again."

"Who are these people?" asked John. "What do they want from you?"

Sami sucked in his breath. "They are Islamic extremists who want the date of the next shipment from the CDC to Dugway Proving Ground."

"Good God! Do you have any idea what's in the shipment?"

"No, but I can guess. John, I reported this to the CDC. I don't know why they ignored it, probably politics, as always. I'll deal with them later. Now I'm going to Duck. I know where the house is and Karen should be safe there. Is Mira all right?" he added, his voice breaking again.

"She's fine," John assured him. "We haven't told her anything. Don't worry, I have a shotgun. I've never killed anyone, but I wouldn't hesitate if any of those bastards show up here."

"We'll find them," Sami promised, "And we'll stop them."

Chapter Thirty Nine

Hilton Head Island, SC

Mahmoud crossed the dark parking lot and ambled up the walk to the embarkation center. Huge oaks blocked out the sky. Low shrubs, clustered around the building, greeted him with a heavy sweet fragrance. The wooden porch creaked beneath him as he mounted the steps, and the door groaned as he pulled it open.

The room smelled of fresh paint and was cool after the humid night. Soft lighting illuminated antique paintings and tasteful period furniture. From behind a low counter, a girl looked up and smiled at Mahmoud. He returned her smile and looked around for a restroom sign.

Inside the small room, he rinsed off his face, dried his hands and checked his watch. It was 9:15 pm The wife had parked her car at 8:45 and should be waiting for the 9:30 shuttle to Daufuskie. Returning to the main room, he saw the girl had left her post and was relieved. Crossing the room in several strides, he exited by the front door.

From the porch, he watched the loose grouping of people waiting at the head of the dock. Two tow-headed children were darting across the grass and chasing fireflies. He pictured his little sisters, rummaging through the rubble of their house back in Beirut, searching for the body of their father and brothers. These Americans existed in a dream world, a cocoon that buffered them from the violence and mayhem that ruled in his country — indeed in most parts of the world.

The blonde children spun in circles around the dimly

lit lawn. Suddenly the little girl squealed and dropped to the
grass. Her laughing brother joined her, playing at some childish
game. "So innocent," Mahmoud thought. "But so were his little
sisters and brothers and it did not protect them."

Scanning the group again, he was unable to identify the
wife. A sign sat in front of the entrance to the dock, so she could
not have entered the boat. He glanced again at his watch, 9:20.
A slender black man, in a white uniform, emerged from the
boat and walked up the dock. Removing the sign, he greeted
the passengers, his smile gleaming in the night. Lights on the
dock illuminated each person as they stepped onto the boat,
several older couples, the young family, two teenage boys.
None even resembled Karen.

Could she have doubled back to her car? Perhaps
when he was in the bathroom. Mahmoud pulled out his cell
and selected Abdullah's number. "She's not here," he told his
partner. "Has she returned to the car?"

"No," said Abdullah, his stomach beginning to churn.
His eyes searched in the dark for any movement around the
silver Lexus. "I told you we should have stayed with her," he
fumed.

Mahmoud ended the call and fished in his pocket for a
cigarette. He pulled out the empty pack and swore. The black
man in the white uniform had paused and was looking back
at the embarkation center as though searching for someone.
Mahmoud stepped back into the shadows and watched until
the gate was closed and the boat chugged away from the
dock. Its windows blinked with yellow lights, their reflection
shimmering atop the dark water.

* * *

Abdullah approached the Lexus SUV, gleaming silver
in the moonlight. He ducked when headlights flashed from the

entrance of the parking lot. They passed over him and the car continued on up the main drive.

Pulling on the driver side door handle of the Lexus, he was surprised to find it unlocked. Entering the car, he quickly pulled the door shut to kill the overhead light. Under his breath, he cursed every female relative of Mahmoud and then added the doctor's wife as a caveat.

The car was clean and empty, as though it had been cleared of the detritus of everyday life. Moving to the back, Abdullah discovered the key fob under the mat. Hearing a crunch of stone nearby, he dropped to the floor then rose carefully to peer out the window.

He exhaled, when he saw Mahmoud's looming form sauntering towards him. Exiting the SUV, he slammed the rear door, and waited. When Mahmoud reached his side, Abdullah thrust out the key fob in his shaking hand.

"Who did she leave this for?" he demanded.

Chapter Forty

I-95 North

Her father's big Mercedes handled well but was unfamiliar. Karen fiddled with the defrost switch, turned the radio on and off, glanced in the rearview mirror and wondered if anyone had followed her.

Checking the green lighted dash, she noted the gas dial had crept down to a quarter tank, and the clock showed it was past midnight. She was still on I-95 heading towards Fayetteville. By her estimation, she was about halfway to Duck.

The initial shock had worn off, and Karen felt drained of all emotion except dread. Trapped in an endless nightmare, she felt completely alone. The freeway signs flashed by like sign posts to a normal world that had vanished. Trees and shrubs humped along the side of the road like the mythical beasts at the Boneyard Beach. That was another lifetime ago.

Sighting a sign for a truck stop, she watched for the bank of overhead lights that finally appeared a mile up the road. Pulling off on the exit, she reduced her speed and checked the rearview mirror. No car had pulled off behind her.

Easing up to a gas pump under the well lit canopy, she located her wallet and slipped out a credit card before remembering Joe's warning. Fumbling in the cash pocket she found twenty-six dollars. Damn! Maybe there was an ATM. But that would be just as bad as a credit card, wouldn't it? Karen's eye fell on the compartment in the dash that would normally hold an ashtray. She pressed the faux wood door and it popped open. Thank God her father always kept cash for emergencies.

He used to joke it was his mobile ATM. She counted out five crisp twenty dollar bills.

She walked to the small booth where an overweight woman with bright yellow hair was chewing gum and reading a magazine. The woman looked up when Karen reached the window and slid three bills into the metal tray under the glass. The cashier pawed the money and turned on the pump without uttering a word. Karen thanked her. "Uh huh," the woman replied, returning to her magazine.

Karen felt better having a full tank of gas and pulled into a parking spot in front of the restaurant where the lighting created an artificial daylight. A bell rang when she entered, and a young bearded man in a green turban greeted her with a smile. She tried to smile back and asked him for directions to the restroom.

"Go to the back and then follow to the right," he said in a sing-song accent. She passed a rack of garish souvenirs: plaster lighthouses, iridescent conch shells, and an array of colorful china starfish. It reminded her of Mira, and she hurried to the restroom.

Hunching in the stall, she hugged herself, pressing a wad of toilet paper against her face. After the wave of grief subsided, she dried her eyes, rinsed her face with cold water, and adjusted the clamp that held her fall of hair.

Sliding into a blue vinyl booth away from the windows, Karen accepted a menu from the waitress. The girl was heavy with a broad pleasant face. "Can I get you something to drink?" she asked. Something in her hazel eyes expressed sympathy.

"Black coffee, please" Karen answered, holding up the menu to hide her face. She had no appetite but hadn't eaten since morning and was starting to feel faint. Settling on a bowl of vegetable soup, she set down the menu and surreptitiously studied the dozen or so patrons who slouched in the surrounding booths. They looked like truck drivers or weary travelers, bleary eyed and focused on the food in front of them.

The waitress had moved on to a table across the room. She was laughing with a burly customer dressed in black leather and sporting a gold hoop earring and a dirty blond pony tail.

A regular? Or was the girl just bored? Several customers were talking on cell phones or punching in text messages.

Karen reached into her purse and fingered her cell. "Sami," she thought.

Chapter Forty One

Savannah, GA

Khalid watched as Sami was approached by the two FBI agents. The conversation was brief and to his relief, the doctor headed back to his car.

Staying low, Khalid squinted through the dark as Sami manipulated his Blackberry. They should have had a way to bug the doctor's car for sound. He had been given a mission but not sufficient tools. He fumed silently at The Teacher. Abdullah and Mahmoud troubled him as well, especially Mahmoud with his dreamy eyes and lazy smile. Even so, judging from the expression on the doctor's face as he returned to his car, the men had done their job well. Khalid would get the details from them later.

The doctor's black BMW rumbled to life and slid into the street, making a tight turn and heading into traffic. Relying on his tracking screen, Khalid followed at a distance. He was surprised when the car passed the turn-off towards Hilton Head and headed north instead. This was strange and troubling.

He punched the button for Mahmoud, who answered on the third ring. "Where are you?" Khalid demanded.

"At the embarkation parking lot. We are next to the wife's car."

"Did she return to Daufuskie?" The long pause told him everything.

"Forget her," Khalid quipped, struggling to keep his voice even. This was not the time to quarrel. "We delivered our message, she is no longer necessary." He silently cursed his lack of information. "The doctor is traveling north, away from Hilton Head. We must follow him."

Mahmoud motioned Abdullah towards their car and slipped the Lexus key into his pocket. If someone wished to follow, he would not make it easy. Khalid described the location where they would rendezvous, and cautioned them, "Do not speed, but do not waste time."

* * *

"Fuck me!" Cartwright exclaimed as he motioned to his partner. "Look at this."

Lugad's dark eyes widened as he scanned the text on Cartwright's Blackberry screen. "Goddamn!" he muttered under his breath. He looked around as if expecting to see the doctor still wandering among the thinning crowd.

"We should have followed him and checked out his car!" Cartwright ran a hand over the short stubble on his head. "Fuck this PC shit!"

"Take it easy. We don't even know if he came in a car. He can't have gone very far."

"Okay, so what? We put out a BOLO for dark, foreign-looking men?"

"Present company excluded," Lugad quipped as he continued reading down the page. "It says the guy's wife is headed to the Outer Banks for a rendezvous with one of our agents. She'll have more information. The guy has to show up somewhere."

"Yeah, well let's make sure it isn't on a plane out of the country," said Cartwright. He shook out his notebook and clicked on his Blackberry. "I'll get this out right away."

Chapter Forty Two

I-95 North

Why? Why? Why? The pathetic mantra looped through Sami's head. Why had he trusted Firth? He knew the career politicians. Why hadn't he trusted Karen? If he had called the FBI maybe..."

"Stop it!" he shook his head as if to clear it. He must get to Karen. Joe would help them. He pictured her entering Sarah's apartment and discovering the body of her friend covered in blood. What kind of savages were these?

Sami had often been uneasy around Sarah. She would jibe and tease him playfully, but he detected an undercurrent of wariness. It frightened him to think her untimely death may have been set in motion by him. He had been a fool, but did that make him guilty? He glanced down at his Blackberry on the passenger seat. *Was Karen afraid of him?*

As though answering his thought, the phone jangled. He clicked the car's speaker.

"Hello?" Silence. "Hello?" Please don't let it be *them*, he thought. How would they get this number?

"Sami." Karen's voice was thin and echoed in the empty space.

He glanced in the rearview mirror and pulled off to the side of the road. "Are you all right?" he asked, shifting the car into park and flicking on his hazards.

"No," Karen answered, "I shouldn't be calling you."

"Karen, I won't let anything happen to you, I swear by my eyes. I love you," his voice broke off.

"I'm not supposed to talk long." Sami heard the catch in her voice.

"I know," he agreed. "Your father told me everything. I'm on my way to Duck now. We'll do whatever Joe tells us to do."

"I know you're innocent, but why couldn't you trust me?"

"I was a fool, but I had reasons. We'll talk when I get there."

"I know," she said. "I need you to be here. I love you."

"I love you, *Habibti*, I love you." Sami continued to whisper the words in Arabic, "*Ana bahebik, bahebik, bahebik…*"

Chapter Forty Three

Ramallah, West Bank of Israel
1993

Sami sat up straight on the edge of his chair in front of the principal's desk. The man was studying a paper that Sami knew would direct the course of his future.

The competition for the scholarship had been fierce but finally winnowed down to a pair of students, Sami Nasser and Ahmad Jalali. The boys had been rivals throughout their high school years and traded back and forth the honor of top student. Now the final judgment day had arrived. Only one would receive the scholarship to attend Emory University in the United States.

Final exams had been agony. No matter how much Sami studied, he would awaken in the night with a feeling of dread. Had he truly understood his father's tutoring? Should he have practiced more? Self-doubt swirled in his brain and blocked out sleep.

At last the principal looked up. Removing his glasses, he wiped them with a white handkerchief while Sami tried in vain to read his expression. When the man finally finished his task, he looked up with the hint of a twinkle in his eye. Sami held his breath and clutched the edges of his chair.

"I'm sure you understand how difficult this decision was for the school. But we have made a selection and the scholarship is yours if you wish to accept it."

"*Mabruk!*" continued the principal as he stood and held out his hand. Sami stayed in his chair for a moment, mouth open, looking up at the man. Then he jumped up as if he'd received an electric shock.

"*Shukran!*" he cried, "*Shukran!*" as he grasped and pumped the outstretched hand.

* * *

When he exited the principal's office, Sami paused and looked down the hallway of his high school. All the sounds and sights were familiar, but he saw them with new eyes and ears. His world was forever altered with a single sentence. *The scholarship is yours.*

He noticed a figure perched on the bench a few yards down from where he stood. His rival, Ahmad, held a book in his lap. He closed it slowly as he searched Sami's face. Their eyes met and in an instant, both knew that nothing needed to be said.

Ahmad rose slowly, set down his book, and held out his hand. "I believe I should congratulate you?" It was more a statement than a question, but a glimmer of hope still shone in the young man's dark eyes.

"Thank you," responded Sami and watched the glimmer fade and die. He flinched. "It could just as easily have been you. I wish it could be both of us."

Smiling sadly, Ahmad shook his head. A shaft of light from the overhead fixture glanced off his glasses. He was shorter than Sami, with a slight build and the intelligent face of a scholar. Sami studied him now, took in the immaculate but well worn clothes and shoes. He knew Ahmad's family was not wealthy and donations were needed to cover a good part of his tuition.

"No," said Ahmad. "There must be one who excels. That is the way the world works. I wish it had been me. But that was not written so I am glad it is you." The words came from Ahmad's heart. He'd been a stranger in the school from the first day he arrived, painfully aware of his status as a charity student.

But he was smart and very proud when he received the highest grade on a math quiz. Afterwards, he recalled Sami swiveling in his seat to look back. The tall, handsome boy scrutinized him before breaking into a wide smile. They sought each other out that afternoon during the lunch break. The boys had little in common as far as background, but their passion for learning forged an unspoken bond between them.

Sami looked at his friend now and nodded, unable to speak. He knew the words were true but wished with all his heart he could change them.

* * *

Sami's father beamed with pride, and his mother immediately set about preparations to slaughter a lamb and plan a feast for family and friends. The weeks rushed by in a flurry of preparation. He was fitted for clothes and shoes and wondered if his jeans would look like the ones Americans wore. He read everything he could find on Emory University and the history of Atlanta and practiced his English in front of the mirror.

The night before his departure finally arrived, but it still did not seem real. Nabil played the *oud* and sang until his voice grew hoarse and tears threatened to choke his words. Amira could not restrain herself and wept openly with her mother and sisters. Staying by Sami's side, Kamal teased his older brother and refilled his plate until Sami could eat no more.

He excused himself to use the restroom, but when he had exited to the hall, he headed for the kitchen instead. He stepped out onto a small verandah off the back of the house. Grateful for the fresh air, he drew in a deep breath and looked up at the stars. *Would they look different in America?*

The door sounded behind him, and he turned to see his cousin approach. Bedia was the youngest daughter of his father's brother and a beauty as her name implied. Both knew the family hoped they would marry one day since a union between the children of brothers was encouraged.

"I wanted to say goodbye," she said. "Four years is a long time."

"Yes." He looked down at her heart-shaped face so lovely in the moonlight. "I waited so long for this and now…" he hesitated. "It is happening too fast. I want to stop this night just as it is. Hold it in my hand and never let go." He stretched out his hand and clenched it shut for emphasis.

Bedia smiled. "You can hold it in your heart." She reached out and put a shy hand on his chest. "You will always carry your family and your country here." She would not have been so bold were he not leaving.

"My *beladi*," he replied, covering her hand with his own, "as Abdul Halim sings." Were he not leaving, there would be no cause to be bold.

"Abdul Halim is from a different world that is history now. I think you are destined for the new world, and I fear you will not return." She felt a tremor shoot through her, despite the warm night air.

"I will return," he vowed. "I swear it."

"*Inshallah*, cousin. If it is written."

* * *

That night Sami lay in his narrow bed in the room he had shared with his brother all his life. He stared up at the ceiling, his eyes tracing a crack in the corner that was lit by a shaft of moonlight. This was the last night he would look up at that crack.

"Are you afraid?" His brother's voice came to him from

the other bed.

Sami thought for a while before replying. "Yes."

"I always knew you would go to America. But I used to believe I would go with you. We would become cowboys together."

Smiling at the memory, Sami felt tears sting his eyes. The brothers had never been separated. "I am going to Georgia, not California," he replied. "But you will come and visit me with *Abiy and Emi*. We will travel and see all the things we dreamed about."

"Sometimes I believe that," answered Kamal. "But other times I feel I will never leave this country, like I am rooted in the land."

"What do you want?" asked Sami, raising himself on one elbow. He peered across the room at his brother who was a shadow in the darkness.

"I want to attend Birzeit and become a teacher like our father. But he always looks backward, I want to look forward. It is good to take pride in our past, but we need to build a future, and that will require new ideas and technologies. I wish to be part of that."

Kamal was always the impetuous one, joking and thriving on action. Sami thought he knew everything about his brother, but suddenly realized you can never fully understand another person, no matter how close. He was sorry they had waited so long to have this conversation.

"As do I," answered Sami. "We will go forward, each on our own path, but always together in our hearts. Sleep well, brother."

Chapter Forty Four

Decatur, GA
1993

When Sami first arrived at Emory, he immersed himself in his studies to fight off the overwhelming homesickness. Thanks to his father's discipline, he was used to putting school first. He bought a used bicycle and rode from his classes to the library and then back to the dorm. He liked the insular quiet of the library and stayed most nights until the wee hours. When he finally crawled into bed, he was usually too tired to think of home or family. Sleep obliterated the constant ache of isolation.

The months swirled by in a panorama of new experiences and emotions. Other students smiled at him and were friendly. He returned their overtures politely but remained aloof. His task was to excel and then return home. His father sent money, but Sami felt guilty accepting it. He knew Birzeit University had been closed off and on for years causing a heavy financial burden for the teachers and students alike.

A solution presented itself near the end of Sami's first semester. A young man approached him as he was packing up his books following a physics class.

"*As-salaamu aleikum.*" The young man was tall and thin with a dark complexion contrasted by light hazel eyes. He regarded Sami with an earnest wariness.

"*Wa aleikum as-salaam,*" Sami replied, smiling. It was good to hear his language.

"My name is Ibrahim Nakleh," the man continued in English.

Sami accepted his hand and replied, "I'm Sami Nasser."

He'd spoken with a few other Middle Eastern exchange students but was reluctant to become involved. Many seemed to have political agendas, and he did not have time for politics.

"I have noticed you in class," said Ibrahim, "and you are an excellent student." He watched as Sami continued stuffing his notebooks and papers into the oversized backpack. "I wonder if you would consider tutoring?" he asked.

Sami zipped his bag shut and heaved it to his shoulder. "I had not thought of it," he replied, flashing a look of interest. "I have another class across campus, do you mind walking with me?"

"Of course," answered Ibrahim, shouldering his own pack. The two men were of a height and walked easily together down the bustling hallway.

Ibrahim continued speaking while Sami fished gloves and a blue knit cap out of his jacket pocket. The weather had turned unseasonably cold for Atlanta, and a swirl of snowflakes swept their faces when Sami opened the double doors to the outside.

"I am concerned about the final exam," said Ibrahim. "I would be grateful for any help—I would pay you, of course."

The pair had reached the metal stand where Sami's battered bike was perched between the rungs. Sami stooped and fingered the combination lock on the chain securing it. He looked up at Ibrahim who was bareheaded with random snowflakes collecting in his tightly-curled black hair.

"I have never tutored formally. I aided my father sometimes with younger students back home and helped my brother, but I am not qualified as a teacher."

"You need no formal qualifications, the rate for most tutors is seven dollars an hour. I will pay you ten."

Sami's jaw dropped. He had been offered the minimum wage of $4.61 to wash dishes at a local restaurant. If he could make this kind of money, he could spare his family the expenses he knew well they could not afford.

"It would be at your convenience, of course," urged Ibrahim.

"Can you meet me in the library tomorrow morning? Early."

"Yes, whatever you wish." Ibrahim's pale eyes glowed. "Where is *back home*?" he asked as Sami straddled his bike.

"Ramullah," said Sami. "What about you?"

"Nazareth," Ibrahim replied.

Sami nodded as he pulled on his gloves and then grasped the handle bars. "I will meet you in the Woodruff Library tomorrow at 6:00 am, *Inshallah*."

"*Inshallah*," echoed Ibrahim as he watched Sami peddle off, head down, legs churning. He pulled his black wool coat tighter across his chest, suddenly aware of the biting wind. And he wondered if Sami had guessed that he was Christian.

* * *

The Woodruff Library was nearly empty on Friday morning at 6:00 am. Ibrahim was waiting for Sami. His physics book and a tablet of yellow lined paper were neatly arranged before him, along with several sharpened pencils.

Sami smiled his approval and sat down across from Ibrahim. The cold had brought a dusky rose hue to his cheeks, and his dark eyes sparkled.

"He is as handsome as he is intelligent," thought Ibrahim. "A rare combination."

The two young men became friends, discovering they shared similar experiences growing up in the "Occupied Territories." Both came from educated families, though Ibrahim was Christian with an Armenian mother. Sami was fascinated by his friend's description of relations between the two major religions in Nazareth. Ibrahim believed the common links between Christianity and Islam were apparent in his town more than in most parts of the region.

"We all pray to the same God," Ibrahim argued. The gospel teaches to love thy neighbor while Muhammad requires respect for people of the book. We do not have to be enemies."

Sami was reminded of his father and agreed with Ibrahim. Family and tradition had ruled their lives since childhood, but the rise of fundamental Islam alarmed both young men. Despite its dependence on technology, the movement sought to drag society back to the violence and superstition of medieval times.

When Sami read about girls prevented from attending school, he was reminded of Amira's intellect and how it had guided her children. Ibrahim's mother worked as a doctor at the English hospital. How would the Middle East fare in the twenty-first century if it continued to devalue half its population?

Sami's reputation grew as a tutor, and he soon had to turn away prospective clients. He took on as many as his grueling schedule allowed, and he discovered that the human contact was slowly filling the gaping hole of loneliness that had plagued him for so many months.

* * *

After completing his undergraduate degree in Biology, Sami was accepted into the medical school. He quickly distinguished himself while continuing his tutoring. During his last year, Sami discovered his passion lay in the field of neurology. The first time he heard Dr. John Cameron lecture, Sami affirmed his choice and was ecstatic when accepted to do post-graduate training with the doctor as his mentor.

Sami had planned to return home after graduating medical school. His family expected him to come home to Ramallah, but it was something he could not do. The opportunity offered him at Emory was too incredible to turn down. He tried to explain in long letters to his parents who begged him to return for a visit, at least. He knew if he looked his father in the face, he would be unable to hide the niggling fear that gnawed at his heart. He could never live in Ramallah again. He promised to return home when he finished his residency and banished the difficult decision to the future.

The incident that would seal his fate occurred at a back-yard barbeque hosted by his mentor. Five other residents attended the event held at Dr. Cameron's historic home in Decatur. Three were male and two female.

Sami surveyed the manicured lawn and sculptured shrubs as he waited on the front stoop. It was warm, and he had opted for neatly pressed khakis and a white shirt. He rang the bell a second time before a woman arrived at the door. Her eyes crinkled as she smiled and invited him inside. Sami judged her to be in her fifties but she was still slender and had clearly been a beauty in her youth.

"You must be one of John's new residents," she said, holding the door open for him. "I'm Alice, his wife."

Sami was slightly ill at ease thinking of the brilliant Dr. Cameron as *John*, but he smiled back and took her outstretched right hand. "It's a pleasure, ma'am. My name is Sami Nasser."

"How sweet of you," said Alice as her eyes fell on the bouquet of red tulips he clutched in his other hand. Accepting the flowers, she paused to sniff the bright petals. "These are just lovely."

She looked past his shoulder at the front window behind him. "I see we have more guests," she said, watching as two more young men approached. "If you'll excuse me…"

A burst of laughter wafted in from the rear of the house. "Everyone is out back," Alice added and gestured in the direction of the sound. "Please, make yourself at home."

"Thank you, ma'am," Sami replied. He noted the high ceilings, dark gleaming floors, and antique furniture as he

walked through the front room towards the kitchen. He had
been invited into the homes of friends and clients, and he was
familiar with the wealth and comfort of life in America. But
this was special. A grand piano dominated one corner of the
room. Several photos sat atop it next to a tall vase of white calla
lilies. Not wanting to pry, Sami continued through the room
and passed a den on his right. He glimpsed a beautifully carved
mahogany desk backed by an enticing wall of books.

At the kitchen, he paused and surveyed the counters
displaying an array of platters and bowls filled with chips,
cheeses, spreads and sliced vegetables. Late afternoon sun
poured through the bay windows and framed a round oak
table. Beyond, Sami saw a lush green yard with a pool nestled
in the center.

He passed through French doors that led to the screened
porch. The room was octagonal and filled with comfortable
wicker furniture. A pair of ferns in wrought iron planters
flanked a stone fireplace. Fat ivory candles, along with several
books and magazines, adorned the tables. Pillows were strewn
in disarray across the couches and chairs. It was clearly a lived
in room.

Sami exited through the screen door to the patio. The
two female residents were seated at a round teak table under
a dark green umbrella. Each held a drink in her hand. The
one named Ruth waved at him. She was heavy with a round,
plain face, but had intelligent dark eyes that sparkled when she
smiled. The other resident, named Anne, was attractive with
smooth blonde hair and even features. Sami sensed her interest
in him, though nothing had been said.

He turned his attention to the third resident, George,
who stood next to Dr. Cameron — *John* — at the grill. He joined
them and was enthusiastically welcomed.

"Good to see you Sami," said his mentor, setting down
a tray of hors d'oeuvres and holding out his right hand. He

sported a red apron that covered the front of his khakis and blue polo shirt. Sunlight winked off his glasses. Sami began to relax.

"Help yourself to a drink," John continued, pointing to a large copper bucket filled with ice and an array of beverages. "And we have plenty of food so don't be shy."

Two more residents joined the group and were greeted warmly by John. Sami knew both Bill and Irving. They had all competed for the coveted slots at Emory and held a mutual respect for each other.

Sami selected a can of Diet Coke from the bucket and flipped the pop top while Bill and Irving grabbed bottles of Heineken.

Alice arrived carrying a crystal vase containing the tulips. Setting it on the table, she arranged the gracefully drooping blossoms and smiled at Sami. "Thank you again," she said, "It was very thoughtful."

"My pleasure, ma'am," he replied, returning her smile. He had worried about what to bring. In his culture no guest would visit another's home empty handed. Candy and honey laden sweets were traditional gifts, but they seemed inappropriate in this situation so he settled on the flowers. It seemed he made the right choice.

The group chatted about sports, school, latest medical news, and eventually food. John loved to cook and enjoyed cuisine from around the world. He engaged Sami in a conversation about Middle Eastern food and was pleased to learn that the young man had a similar interest. Sami described his initial attempts to duplicate the familiar food from his homeland. His first attempt at falafel produced charred little nuggets that were hard enough to be used as weapons. The hummus was laced with so much garlic he avoided getting close to anyone for two days. John was pleased to see Sami laughing. The young man had always seemed so reserved and serious.

As the sun was going down, Alice began lighting candles. The guests helped her return trays to the kitchen and came back carrying bowls of beans and salads. John checked the corn on the cob that had been put on the grill to roast and determined it was time to start the shrimp and burgers.

"Is there anything I can do to help sir?" asked Sami.

"Well, yes, while I season the burgers you can butter the buns," said John, pointing to a nearby mound of bread.

"I usually put a little butter on to help them brown," he explained as he arranged a row of thick red patties and several skewers of shrimp on the grill. Sami was concentrating on slathering butter across the spongy white rolls when John raised his hand and shouted, "Hey kiddo!"

Looking up, Sami stared and froze, butter knife mid-air. He was instantly transported back to the darkened cinema where he beheld the angelic face of Faten Hamama for the first time. He felt the same lurch in his gut, almost a physical pain. The slender young woman who approached was dressed casually in an ivory skirt and a white sleeveless blouse. Her dark hair fell in waves about her shoulders and framed a face of exquisite beauty.

"How are you Dad?" she asked, tumbling into John's embrace. "I'm sorry to be so late."

"No problem, I'm just glad you made it." John turned to Sami. "Let me introduce you to one of my new residents, Sami Nasser. Meet my daughter, Karen."

Sami dropped the knife he was holding and noticed a glob of butter clinging to his hand.

"Ma'am. Excuse me," he said fumbling for a napkin to wipe off the greasy substance. Karen retracted her hand and laughed. "Don't worry about it. I see Dad's put you to work."

Sami forgot about the butter, the towel, and the bread as he stared into the clearest green eyes he had ever seen.

"Do you need me to do anything Dad?" asked Karen,

turning to her father.

"No honey, we're good here, but your mom can probably use some help."

"Okey dokey," she said and flashed another look at Sami. "Nice to meet you."

"My pleasure," he replied and watched her walk back across the lawn. He turned back to buttering the buns and mechanically arranging them on the grill. He was trying desperately to make sense of what just happened when he smelled burning bread and grabbed the long spatula to rescue buns before they were ruined. John watched with concealed humor. He'd seen the way men reacted to his daughter since she turned thirteen.

Sami wasn't aware of what he ate or of what conversations he had. He felt like an actor on stage, reading someone else's lines and performing their actions.

The only reality was her. He stole glances down the table and noticed that Karen laughed easily and listened more than she spoke. After the meal, she helped her mother clear the table. He followed her form covertly and looked away when she caught his eye.

When dessert was served, Sami accepted a plate holding a large portion of chocolate cake. He didn't want to be rude but knew he wouldn't be able to swallow it. Karen had poured herself a glass of white wine and came to sit beside him. She kicked off her sandals and tucked one long leg beneath her. In a smooth gesture, she brushed a sweep of glossy hair behind her ear. The bare flesh of her lightly tanned arms was smooth and glowed in the candlelight.

"You should try the cake," she said. "It's my mom's secret recipe."

"I'm sure it's wonderful," he replied, "but you see, I don't eat chocolate." *What an idiotic thing to say. Was he losing his mind?*

Karen raised her eyebrows. "Really? Neither do I. However, my Dad's a chocoholic. Would you like something else to drink?"

"Thank you, but I am good," he replied and gestured to the bottle of Heineken on the table beside him.

She glanced down into her wine glass. "If I'm not being rude, may I ask where you're from?"

"Ramallah. It's on the West Bank of Israel. I came to the US on a scholarship." *God, how pompous and ridiculous that must sound!* His brain was screaming at him.

"I've always wanted to go there," said Karen. "Sacred to three great religions, it must be a special place."

She was so close he could smell her light perfume and see the candle flame dancing in those hypnotic eyes. Religion was the furthest thing from his mind as he realized with horror that his groin was stirring. Willing it down only heightened his arousal. He felt beads of sweat forming on his forehead. Scooping up a discarded napkin, he wiped his face and then casually dropped it in his lap.

"Warm night," he said.

Karen favored him with an enigmatic smile and took a sip of her wine. "Yes, isn't it."

Chapter Forty Five

I-95 North

Sami checked his speedometer and eased his foot off the gas. The hours crawled by in an endless night. His car passed through pockets of fog that writhed up from the asphalt like shadowy fingers. The drizzle had started up again setting off his wipers that arced across his windshield, back and forth, back and forth. He was glad he had bought a large coffee when he stopped for gas in Fayetteville.

Glancing in the rearview mirror, Sami was relieved to see the car he thought had been following him was gone.

Karen's voice still rang in his ears while images of her and Mira swam before his face. He wondered where the terrorists were. That was the word he used now, and he was sure there were more than one. How many? How many does it take to slaughter a small woman? What sort of twisted mind construes murder as an act of glory?

Sami thought of his younger brother. Kamal could no more have been aligned with these animals than he could spread wings and fly. His brother was angry, dissatisfied, and impetuous, but he was not evil. These men were evil.

How long since he had last been home? Three years?

Chapter Forty Six

Ramallah, West Bank of Israel
2007

Mira had been two the second time Sami returned to
Ramallah to introduce his bride and daughter. The little girl
had captivated everyone, especially her grandmother. Kamal
was newly married and his wife, Nejla, welcomed them with
warmth and charm.

Amira was still wiry: her piercing eyes alert and
questioning. She had always run her household with a jealous
hand, and even her husband knew better than to question her on
domestic matters. Sami was surprised to see Amira now defer
to Nejla as the "woman of the house". When he teased her about
it, she shrugged and replied, "I grow tired sometimes. Nejla is
young and strong." He read the resignation in his mother's eyes
and though it pained him he respected her wisdom.

Nabil had aged more dramatically. His foot and leg
gave him unrelenting pain, and he used a cane now to walk. His
beloved *oud* gathered dust in a corner. Arthritis had stiffened
his fingers, and he could no longer coax out the lovely notes.
Neither son had inherited his musical gift.

Sami shared a pot of coffee with his father one morning
on their balcony beneath the shade of a lemon tree. Pots of
herbs and flowers clustered along a low wall, their perfume
permeating the early morning air. The potent scent of cardamom
wafted from the brass pot on the wicker table between them.
Sami picked up his small handle-less cup from the tray while
his father carefully did the same with some difficulty. Sami
averted his eyes.

Father and son toasted and then savored the rich, dark liquid. "God is good," they agreed.

"I have missed you *Abiy*," said Sami. "It is good to see you."

Nabil smiled taking another sip of coffee. "You could come home," he suggested, eying the son who was his mirror image at the same age.

Sami shook his head. "It is not so easy," he replied. "I've worked hard to achieve my position, and I think my work is important. I believe what I do is good."

His father nodded. "I understand. We are proud of you. But you can also do good here."

Sami set his cup down and ran a hand through his hair. "Ramallah is so different now. I honestly don't know if I could come home again. And I must think of Karen and Mira."

Nabil considered, also settling his cup on the tray. He gestured for Sami to pour them another serving. "Your wife and child will follow you, as they should." Touching his chest he continued, "But you, *Ibni*, must follow your heart."

* * *

Kamal bristled when Sami brought up the subject of their father later that evening. The two brothers shared a table in an outside café. Heat from the day cloaked the still air and mingled with the smells of roasting meat and sizzling falafel.

"You don't remember how stubborn he is," said Kamal. "He speaks out in the mosque on Friday against Hamas. Do you know how dangerous that is?"

Clamping a cigarette between his lips, he leaned forward in his chair to use the candle as a lighter. "The only reason we haven't been attacked is that I pretend he is senile."

He inhaled and then blew a puff of smoke adding, "He may well be, you know."

Sami pointed to the discarded pack of smokes. "Those will kill you."

Kamal snorted, "If the Israelis or Muslim Brotherhood don't get me first."

A young man appeared at their table to take their order. Sami glanced down at the menu and ordered a beer. Raising his eyebrows, Kamal asked for a glass of mint tea along with an order of mezza for them to share. "So," he said, "You drink now?"

"Occasionally," Sami responded and gestured towards the cigarette pack. "We choose our own poison."

"Ah, but mine is not forbidden," quipped Kamal.

"That's because it was invented after the Prophet lived, Peace be Upon Him."

Kamal just shook his head, knowing the argument would go nowhere.

"What do you think of Hamas?" Sami asked.

Looking both ways, Kamal lowered his voice. "It is not wise to discuss politics in public places. You have been away too long, brother."

"Perhaps," said Sami. Their drinks arrived followed by the food. The table was soon laden with plates of appetizers including spiced meatballs, fried cauliflower, hummus with olive oil, pickled turnips, and tomato salads.

Breaking off a piece of warm pita bread, Sami scooped up a clump of garlic laced eggplant dip.

He closed his eyes, letting the smoky flavor melt in his mouth before swallowing. "We have many restaurants that serve Arabic food in the U.S." he said. "But it never tastes like this, no matter how much you pay."

"Of course not," Kamal agreed. "The food is grown on our ancestral land. It is a part of us. Do you know we had a film festival here in Ramallah?" he continued. "It was the first event held in the new cultural center. Eighty films from around the world were shown, including 25 by Palestinian directors."

"I remember," Sami smiled, "And I was very proud."

The meal stretched out across the evening while the brothers laughed and talked of their families, their childhood, and the new technologies and music. They ordered another pot of mint tea.

"Just don't become an infidel in that decadent country," warned Kamal with a smile.

"That could never happen," said Sami. "We have Bedouin blood, as our mother has reminded us since we were born. Blood is always true."

Chapter Forty Seven

Outer Banks, NC

The bridge to Manteo was just ahead. This was the third bridge Karen would cross within the last eleven hours. She shifted in her seat trying to stretch her back. Her eyes burned. The coffee had kept her wired but concentration was a problem. The reflection of the full moon on the Croatan Sound dredged up so many memories.

Sami had been captivated from his first glimpse of the Outer Banks. After their summer visit to Sarah and John's place in Duck, he immediately made plans to return in early fall. It was during his residency, so they stayed in the John Yancey in Kill Devil Hills. It was economical but offered an oceanfront view where they could throw peanuts to the seagulls from their small balcony and watch the moon rise.

Ghosts roamed freely in the time before dawn. They whispered in the whooshing surf and rustled through the windswept scrub. The number of boats and ships lost near the Outer Banks is estimated at over a thousand. The place was aptly dubbed the "Graveyard of the Atlantic."

The tall narrow beach houses of Nags Head loomed up ahead. Legend has it that pirates of the Outer Banks would place a lantern around a "Nags Head" and walk it up and down the sand dunes on the beach to lure trade ships at sea into thinking they were entering a harbor. As a ship got closer to land, it would beach itself like a whale, and the pirates would invade the ship and do what pirates do.

Karen had always been skeptical. "Have you ever tried

to tie anything with fire around a horse's neck?" But Sami was adamant despite his scientific background that some things should not be questioned, local legends among them.

"The Whale's Tale" slid by on her left.

It seemed only yesterday that Sami and she had maneuvered their way through a crowd to the bar. After climbing the famous Cape Hatteras light house in the humidity of a sweltering August day, they were parched for liquid. They had downed three Newcastle ales before their table was ready. Karen recalled sharing fried oysters, steamed shrimp, roasted corn, and hush puppies while snuggling together in a booth overlooking the Albemarle Sound at sunset. Drunk on beer and each other, they teased and laughed and reveled in their mutual arousal.

Anxious to return to their hotel room, Sami ciphered the tab while Karen collected her beach bag. Noticing an elderly couple across from them, she nudged Sami in the ribs. The man was intent on his food but the woman was scowling at them. In answer, Sami pulled Karen up against him and planted a long slow kiss. As they left, Sami gave the woman a smile and a nod while the husband looked up in confusion as his wife hissed in his ear.

Once outside, Sami and Karen burst into laughter and staggered over to the railing to keep their balance.

"I can't believe you did that!" Karen rubbed her eyes. "Oh my God! Did you see her face?"

"Did you see his face?" Sami countered, catching his breath. "That poor guy..." That set them off on another peal of mirth. Straightening up, he put his arm around her. "Come on, we've attracted enough attention. We better get back before they put us in the pokey."

Karen giggled, "The pokey? How do you know words like that?"

Sami shrugged, "I don't know, movies I saw as a kid, or

books. I like funny words. Pokey is funny."

They made their way a little unsteadily to the motel. The small swimming pool was lit, and three children were splashing in the turquoise depths while their parents lounged in chairs. Inside the John Yancey, the couple navigated the sandy hallway and took the stairs to their floor.

Dropping her bag, Karen ran her hands through her windblown hair. "We need a shower," she said.

"I need to pee," Sami responded, "Bad!"

"Ooh, can I watch?"

"It wouldn't work," his standard reply.

Karen crossed the room and opened the sliding door, filling the room with the sound of crashing surf. The moon had risen and cast a path of phosphorescence across the ocean. She heard the water running behind her. Leaving the window open, she pulled the drapes closed and crossed to the bathroom. Peeling off her clothes and underwear, she left them on the floor and pushed open the door.

Sami was already in the shower lathering himself with soap. "This is going to be close," Karen observed, squeezing in behind him. She put her hands on his shoulders, loving the look and feel of them as she massaged the muscles in caressing circles.

"Do you want a back rub?" she asked.

"I'd rather give you a front rub," he said turning to face her. His soapy hands found her small, high breasts. She looked down at the contrast of his brown-gold hands on her white flesh, just below the tan marks.

She sucked in her breath when he gently pinched her nipples, rubbing them between his thumb and forefinger. "Breasts are just breasts," he murmured. "But nipples are wonderful." Rinsing the soap, he bent to suckle the left one." Karen moaned, and leaned back against the tile, bracing herself against the wall.

When he released the pink nodule, she asked, "What about the other one. You don't like it."

"Not true," he said bending to her right breast. "But the left is my favorite."

By the time their soapy hands reached below the waist, they could wait no longer. He hoisted her up in a smooth motion and she locked her legs around his waist. The alcohol had drowned all inhibitions and Karen held nothing back, her voice rising in a shattering crescendo.

Sami teased her later as they cuddled on the bed. "We may be banned from this place forever. I am surprised someone didn't call the police."

They had cracked the drapes so a sliver of moonlight fell across the sheets. She slapped him lightly on the shoulder, "I was not that loud."

"Oh yes you were," he said. "I'll have to give you beer more often."

Karen smiled. It was a perfect end to a perfect day. She knew instinctively, it would be remembered for life, one of those rare moments when you realize it will never be better than this. The ever-present wind of the Outer Banks caught the white sheers at the window and they billowed into the room.

Chapter Forty Eight

Jamesville, NC

Abdullah filled the gas tank while Mahmoud loped to the convenience store to get cigarettes and cold drinks.

"Don't forget Rolaids," called Abdullah, cursing his churning stomach. He had always had trouble, but it was much worse in this cursed land. Looking up at the hazy dark, he thought of the clear night skies of Yemen. The stars blazed there in such profusion and intensity Abdullah felt he was beholding the face of Allah. He wondered if he would ever see his home again in the barren Hadhramout Region. Would he ever breathe the clean air of the mountains or would he die in this wet stinking land with the smell of decay in his nostrils.

He glanced at the shadows on the side of the truck stop where Khalid had parked and was waiting for them. Abdullah knew he was angry. Khalid had not abused them, but his black eyes blazed. Like Abdullah, he had lost weight since the beginning of their mission. His cheekbones protruded above the down-turning lines around his mouth. Abdullah could not recall ever seeing the man smile.

Mahmoud was the opposite extreme. Grinning at every infidel like a baboon. He was shuffling back towards Abdullah now, a cigarette already dangling from his lips. He tossed several small bags in the back seat after pulling out a Pepsi for himself and a small carton of milk for Abdullah. "It will settle your stomach," he said, passing the container to his companion, who grunted his thanks.

"He will probably expect me to let him smoke in the car

for this," thought Abdullah. *"Bismallah, ar-Rahman, ar-Rahim, this would be a long night."*

Mahmoud slid into the driver's seat and started the car. He circled around to the place where Khalid was parked and with a glance at Abdullah, tossed his cigarette out the open window. Khalid was staring intently at the tracking screen in front of him. "He is still driving north," he said, pointing though only he could see the green blip.

"So he is going back to Atlanta?" asked Mahmoud.

"No, he would not use that route," answered Khalid. "He may be following his wife. If she took another car, she may have suspected she was being followed, or she may have been warned."

"Warned by who?" Mahmoud's eyes were wide in the dark, his pupils enlarged.

Khalid bestowed a withering look, "If we had access to their phones, we would know. For now we have no choice but to follow the doctor. Pray to Allah we find them together. It will make our mission much easier."

"Allahu Akbar," his companions agreed.

"Are your weapons ready?" Khalid asked. The two nodded. "Keep one in the car in case you are stopped," he added.

"In the glove box," Mahmoud responded.

"Good. We will stay together. *Yallah.*"

Chapter Forty Nine

Duck, NC

Karen slowed as she approached Duck. They had almost bought a house here a few years back. It was located on the Sound off Ruddy Duck Lane. Nestled back from the road and protected by a cluster of wild oaks, it reminded Karen of Daufuski. Weathered cedar shakes, accented with white trim, blended into the gray of the water behind. Inside, the floors gleamed with hardwoods and a wall of glass looked out over the Currituck Sound. A week before closing, the survey unearthed problems. The dock encroached on a neighbor's property on one side and the sea wall did the same on the other.

They walked away, grateful for avoiding the legal nightmare, and taking it as an omen. Daufuski became their getaway as it always had been for Karen. Sami enjoyed the island and her parents, but she knew he belonged in the Outer Banks. From the untouched sand dunes of Ocracoke to the wild horses that roamed the tip of Corolla, the land spoke to his heart.

As much as she wanted this nightmare to end, she was reluctant to see Joe, to see Sarah's features reflected in his face. "What could she say to him? That she unwittingly led a monster to his sister's house?" She had played the scene over in her head during the long drive. It could have been a robbery, or a jealous fan. But she knew that wasn't true. The ritual slaying and the mutilated paintings were a message, to her and to Sami.

For the hundredth time she pictured the dark sedan she'd noticed as they walked back from the restaurant. If only she had followed her hunch. If only she had said something, warned Sarah. If only...

Karen pulled over when she saw Elizabeth's Café on the right. She recalled the lunches and dinners with Sarah and friends in the flagstone courtyard. The nights of sipping wine and sharing dreams. They were young, blessed by the gods and invulnerable. With fierce persistence and determination, Sarah had achieved her dream to be a professional artist. An image of her friend's body and the desecrated paintings flashed before her. Pressing her hands against her eyes, Karen wept softly. She had thought her tears were dried up but she was wrong.

"Forgive me Sarah, forgive me."

Chapter Fifty

Sami ignored the trucks that roared past him and watched for cars. At one point he thought he was being followed, but the car eventually turned off at an exit. He was almost alone now on the highway. The clock on his dash registered 3:40 am. He should be in Duck by 5:30.

Karen's lovely face floated before him. He would give anything to hear her voice. Know that she was safe. He had failed her in the worst way a husband could. He had put their lives in jeopardy for fear of a politically correct bureaucracy. And Sarah had been the victim, being in the wrong place at the wrong time.

Sami had struggled with his faith for years. Not his belief in God or Islam, but how it was interpreted. From boyhood, he would watch Nabil remove his shoes and shuffle into the masque, his twisted foot on display. As fellow worshipers averted their eyes, Sami hurt for the man, but he also burned with pride at his father's courage.

Nabil was devout and never touched alcohol or pork. He would probably be disappointed in his son. Sami recalled his parents' pride when he had graduated medical school. It was an honor to have the title of doctor, *Al Hakim*, meaning wise man.

His father revered the sciences, just as he abhorred violence. How many men like Nabil were left? It seemed as if their entire culture had been hijacked by the ignorant and the brutal. What was the point of chanting God's *suwar* while slaughtering innocents? The questions swirled in Sami's brain, unanswered.

He pictured the agents who questioned him outside Sarah's house. The suspicion in the tall man's eyes was barely concealed. Sami had experienced it before, in airports and restaurants, even at work. His heritage was plainly written on his face, and he resented that it should engender fear. But he could not blame the West entirely. The usurpers of Islam slaughtered fellow Muslims as much as the reviled infidels — maybe more so.

"Like the animal or animals threatening his family," he thought. "The ones who murdered Sarah. There had to be more than one. Who were they? And where were they now?"

Far behind him a siren wailed splitting the silence. Glancing at the speedometer, Sami quickly eased his foot off the accelerator. He could not afford any delays. He would not fail Karen a second time.

Chapter Fifty One

US-64 E, NC

The car's movement lulled Abdullah to sleep. He dreamt he was a young boy tending his father's goats in Yemen. The tribe's camp was close by, and he could smell spices and fat from the evening meal roasting over the fire. Meat signified visitors. They came and went under the cover of darkness, recruiting men and boys.

At fourteen, Abdullah was old enough to join Al Qaeda, but something caused him to hesitate. He felt close to Allah in his mountains, and he did not wish to leave.

The dying sun hung behind him, its heat already extinguished by the chill sweeping in with night. The sacred crescent of the moon hovered over the cluster of dark tents sprawled out below.

The goats nestled against him for warmth, the smallest nuzzling its soft face against his hand. Shifting his staff, Abdullah clucked and petted the knobby little head as he kept a sharp eye out for jackals. With the other hand, he fingered his dagger tucked into the thick leather belt that held his *futa* in place. The cold was creeping over his sandaled feet and up his bare legs. He unraveled his shawl of woven wool and wrapped it around his thin shoulders.

It would be good to sit around the campfire with his father, uncles and brothers. They would talk, relish the bitter green coffee, and rest from the day's toil. The visitors might be from a neighboring tribe, bearing news. He would recognize them by the cut of their clothing and the manner in which they wrapped their turbans.

He quickened his step and spat out the slimy clump of *qat* he had been chewing through the afternoon to keep up his energy level. The bitter taste remained in his mouth while the scent of mutton wafted to him again. He was famished.

As Abdullah picked his way down the steep slope, the wind whistled around him tinkling the little bells that hung from the goats. He paused on the path, suddenly aware of a distant droning. It reached out across the barren landscape and hummed like some giant insect.

Ahead, he saw figures emerging from the tents. Several of the men pointed to the sky. Abdullah didn't have time to be afraid. The first bombs erupted into balls of flame and shook the ground beneath him. He crouched behind an outcrop of rocks and threw his arms over his head while the world degenerated into a nightmare of thundering explosions, screaming victims, and bleating goats.

* * *

Abdullah swore as he jolted awake from the siren's blare and saw the flashing blue lights reflected in the rearview mirror. "Khalid told you not to speed!" he yelled, drawing on every curse his sleep befuddled mind could conjure.

"I am at the speed limit," Mahmoud answered evenly. "Let me handle this. I know their ways better than you."

Abdullah punched open the glove compartment and passed the gun to Mahmoud who stowed it in the foot well beside the door. After easing the car to the side of the road, Mahmoud lowered the window.

Backlit by his headlights, the highway patrolman looked big as he approached the car, as big as Mahmoud. He was cautious and kept one hand on his gun. When he bent down to peer in the window, his face was rounded and young, his shock of blond hair cut short.

"Is there a problem officer?" Mahmoud asked.

"You have a tail light out," the patrolman said, angling his flashlight from Mahmoud to Abdullah, slouched in the passenger seat. "Were you aware of that?"

"No sir," answered Mahmoud.

"May I see your license please?" the officer continued.

"Of course," answered Mahmoud, pulling his wallet out and handing over the international license Khalid had provided.

The patrolman inspected it and handed it back. "Thank you," he said. "You need to get that tail light fixed right away." His eyes were blue-gray and etched with fatigue.

"Yes sir, we will," answered Mahmoud, smiling as he accepted his license. "Thank you officer."

The patrolman nodded and straightened up. He looked down the road and saw a car parked on the shoulder up ahead. Something was wrong, something he couldn't put his finger on. Bending down again, he saw that Mahmoud had lit a cigarette, the smile still frozen on his face. Abdullah huddled in the dark, his face turned away.

"Would you please open your trunk, sir?" the patrolman asked, but it was not a question.

Mahmoud shrugged. "Sure, whatever you say," he replied, taking a draw from his cigarette and tossing it out the window. He shifted in his seat as if searching for the button to pop the trunk, at the same time swinging up his weapon. He registered the shock on the patrolman's face as the man stepped back and reached for his pistol. Too late.

The blast reverberated across the deserted highway. The patrolman staggered backwards, a blossom of red spreading across his chest. He clawed at the wound, as though trying to remove it. Mahmoud exited the car and stood over the man, observing the look of confusion on his face as he crumpled to the pavement.

"Is he dead?" asked Abdullah from the depths of the passenger seat.

"Yes," replied Mahmoud, pumping another round into the man at his feet. "He is dead."

* * *

Khalid slammed his car into reverse and came screeching back to the scene. He braked just in front of the sedan and jumped out.

"Allah save us, what have you done?" Khalid stared at the patrolman's body, sprawled on the road, blood still seeping from the wounds in his chest. Then he looked at Mahmoud whose expression was calm. The blue police lights pulsed behind him, glinting off the gun, now hanging down in his right hand.

"I had no choice," said Mahmoud. "He asked me to open the trunk. We have a taillight out. It was bad luck." He gave his characteristic shrug.

Frantically searching the highway, Khalid glanced back at Abdullah who had come to stand beside his partner. "Turn off the police lights!" Khalid hissed at him. "Mahmoud, turn out your car lights and get the body off the road. Thanks be to Allah we are not on the interstate." Getting back in his car, Khalid pulled in front of the second sedan and parked.

Mahmoud grunted as he dragged the dead weight of the patrolman's body to the side of the highway and rolled it into a ditch. He was sweating when he returned to watch Abdullah searching for the switch to kill the blue lights.

All three froze when they saw headlights and heard a vehicle approaching. Without a word, Mahmoud and Khalid ducked out of sight, while Abdullah slammed the car door shut and looked away.

A white pick-up truck slowed as it approached the scene, then sped up after passing.

Khalid exited his car and stood shaking as he watched the receding red tail lights winking in the dark until they disappeared. Abdullah succeeded in shutting off the police lights, but the squawking and crackle of the radio shattered the silence.

"This is very bad," said Khalid, looking down at the blood streaked asphalt.

"It could be blood from an animal," offered Mahmoud. "But we should drive the police car off the road."

"Police cars have trackers and they will come when he doesn't answer his radio. But that may give us some time." Khalid's voice was shrill and his eyes haunted as they darted up and down the road.

"Abdullah, drive into that field and park behind the trees. Quickly! And be sure to wipe anything you touched." Khalid knew that no FBI or CIA database would contain the Yemeni's prints, but that was no reason to be careless.

Abdullah complied and soon joined his companions back on the highway. He stooped to retrieve the discarded cigarette butt. Shaking his head at Mahmoud, he held it between his index finger and thumb and made a show of dropping it into the large cupped hand.

Khalid cursed them both for fools. "Get in your car and follow me. We are losing time. Go! *Emshi!*"

Chapter Fifty Two

Duck, NC

The stunted live oaks gave way to low scrub and sand as Karen drove out of downtown Duck. The Currituck Sound gleamed behind the dark beach houses on her left, a conglomeration of buildings that ranged from weather beaten shanties to glitzy oversized rentals with swimming pools and whimsical names.

The Outer Banks was so different from Haig Point, yet it had the same feel. Families came here to escape. Children splashed in the surf, erected sand castles, and collected shells. The sun bleached their hair and gilded their bodies. Mothers swept up sand, washed towels, slathered on sunscreen, and played on the beach with their offspring.

Fathers arrived on the weekends and dragged out the fishing gear and golf clubs. By evening, the sprawling porches were dotted with clusters of friends and neighbors. The smell of fried fish and roasting corn blended with salt air and seaweed. Teak tables creaked under platters of coleslaw, potato salad, buttered hush puppies, and micro-brewed beer. When the sun finally slid beneath the horizon, children were bathed and put to bed where they whispered until sleep overtook them. Adults lounged in the dark, feet propped on deck rails, cocktails or wine in hand as their eyes traced the moon and stars.

When Karen reached the narrow part of the island, she turned right onto Norwood Drive and drove up the hill. Pausing at the top, she looked back at the smooth mirror of the Sound and then forward at the churning Ocean. So fragile, this

strip of land caught between two bodies of water. She lowered
the car window and breathed deeply, letting the wind wash
over her face. It whistled through the car, barely audible above
the drum beat of the surf.

Driving down the hill, she turned right again on Swallow
Lane and spotted the house at the end of the road. It squatted
among the scrub, dark and sprawling, backlit by the moon
washed beach. Karen eased into the driveway, and saw Joe's
silver Porsche, crouched like a giant insect under the spindly
poles supporting the house. A watery yellow light streamed
from one window above her.

* * *

Joe checked his Blackberry and glanced at his watch. He
hadn't heard from Lois since she filled him in on the Savannah
agents' encounter with Sami. She told him a BOLO had gone
out in case the doctor headed for an airport. It was a necessary
precaution, but to Joe, a waste of time. If Karen was right, Sami
would be in as much danger as she. The bureau would track
him down once Karen was brought in and provided the vital
details they needed.

The house was quiet except for the old clock in the hall
ticking out the minutes. Pulling off his glasses, he pinched the
bridge of his nose and pictured the absurd image of a giant
hour glass.

Tick. Tick. Tick.

*A private plane crash in the Adirondacks takes the lives of
Virginia senator, Gerald Miles and his wife Sylvia.*

Tick. Tick. Tick.

Celebrated artist murdered in her Savannah loft.

Clouds bunched overhead, obliterating the stars and
moon. Turning away from the bank of windows and the
relentless surf, Joe wiped his eyes with a handkerchief and

replaced his glasses. The desk lamp illuminated the painted bookshelves across from him. "All the days of our lives," he murmured inspecting the collection of photos.

A young Sylvia smiled back at him. She reclined under an umbrella and sported huge Audrey Hepburn sunglasses. Brushing her blond hair back from her face, she appeared to be laughing. Gerald's photos were mostly action shots, deep-sea fishing, shooting skeet, schmoozing with buddies. His broad Irish face was handsome and topped by a thatch of wavy auburn hair.

The family photos were stilted by comparison. The subjects stood or sat, posed with frozen smiles—except for Sarah. She managed to look pissed in every one. He bent closer and couldn't help but smile at the tiny girl perched on her father's knees, eyebrows drawn down, fists curled in her lap. A bright yellow sundress set off her mass of orange-red curls.

He studied his own visage in the photo. The obligatory smile stretched across his lean sun-browned face as he stood next to his mother. A casual hand draped across her shoulder. Moving on to photos of Sarah and himself, he was amazed at how candid they were.

Like the photos of his father, the majority were action shots. Running along the wide beach with kites, knotted tails trailing across a faded blue sky. Digging for ghost crabs in the sand dunes. Sarah chewing a clam, her eyes wide and cheeks bulging. He remembered watching the grill with her and waiting for the clams to pop open. As soon as one cooled enough, she would stuff it into her mouth and chew greedily. Sylvia was afraid she would choke but Gerald only laughed.

He picked up a photo of the two children sitting on the back steps and peering into a bucket that sat between them. He had no idea what it might have contained. Both were grinning, as if caught in the midst of some joke. Their heads were bent together, her hair a halo of flame against his darker, burnished copper.

He ran a hand through that hair now, picturing his mother, thin and nervous. But the woman who took these photos reveled in the movement and colors of life. He couldn't remember that woman. The years had washed her away leaving a ghost in her stead.

Was that what had driven Sarah? Fear of having her talent and fire extinguished? Though she scoffed at his mundane existence, she had always confided in him. He was the brother who whispered with her in the dark to ward off the outside world. The world where Sylvia hid her tears along with the vodka bottle in the kitchen cupboard. The world where Gerald hid his rages and infidelities from his constituents, but not his family.

Tick. Tick. Tick.

Sarah is gone.

Chapter Fifty Three

Outer Banks, NC

"Karen should be in Duck now," thought Sami. He fought the urge to call her. He glanced at the clock on his dash and estimated dawn would come soon. Though it brought no hint of light, he could feel its presence, as if the world held its breath waiting for darkness to retreat.

Memories washed over him as he pulled onto the bridge. Karen had told him the windswept sand dunes brought out the Bedouin in him. She was right. He could picture a camel plodding across the barren terrain, especially along the isolated stretch of National Seashore leading to Ocracoke Island.

Karen understood him as no one else ever would. Yet even she could not know how it felt to be an outsider in your own country, as well as in the place of your birth. The Americans were wary of his Arab roots, while the Arabs distrusted his American citizenship.

Sami recalled the first time he and Karen came to the Outer Banks as guests of the Miles family. Gerald had been the perfect host, taking them golfing, sailing, and trap shooting.

Karen excelled in all three, but her prowess at shooting impressed Sami the most. He had never shot a gun before. Few Israeli Arabs were authorized to possess a firearm and penalties for breaking the law were draconian.

Joe and Sami had dragged the trap machine from the garage to the beach while Gerald selected the shotguns.

Sami listened with fascination as Karen loaded a Browning Citori 20 gauge while parroting her father's instructions memorized long ago.

"You have about one second after calling to identify the target's angle and break it. Your gun needs to point exactly where you are looking. Watch me," she added with a smile.

Raising the Browning to her face, Karen squeezed her eyes shut, then opened them. Satisfied with the alignment, she called for the target.

"Pull!"

A clay pigeon soared out of the trap and exploded a second later about 36 yards out.

"Pull!"

A second clay shot out low and met the same fate. Karen reloaded quickly and in one smooth motion, raised her shotgun back in position.

Joe was grinning as he reset the trap. "Here comes the double," he called.

Karen gave him a brief nod. "Pull!"

Two clays shot out simultaneously, one high, the other low.

Boom!Boom! The low one exploded first, then the high.

Sarah whooped. "Damn! This is going to be a contest." She winked at Sami. "Didn't know you were married to Annie Oakley did you?"

Gerald and Sylvia watched from beach chairs set up under a striped canopy. The senator nodded his approval, his eyes tracing Karen's slender limbs as the wind pasted her cotton shirt and shorts against her body. Sylvia smiled and took a sip of her martini. Her eyes absently sought the horizon. She had always hated guns.

While Sarah took her turn, Karen instructed Sami on gun points.

"Don't muscle the gun. Hold it lightly with the fore-end just resting across the palm of your hand, like this." She adjusted his grip. "Raise your head a little and relax your neck muscles."

Sami felt the light stroke of her fingers along the nape of his neck. She told him to close his eyes for a few moments and then open them.

"You should see the two beads directly in line on your ventilated rib." She pointed for emphasis.

His wife never ceased to surprise him.

They all took turns shooting except for Sylvia. Joe and Karen were best, but Sami learned quickly and by the afternoon end amazed everyone by hitting a double.

The day ended with cocktails and a sumptuous dinner at the Sanderling Resort where they toasted a perfect weekend.

* * *

Karen was at ease among Sarah's family, as she was with most people. She chided Sami when he joked about being the token minority. His status as a third-year medical student at Emory impressed Sarah's parents, but he still sensed a subtle reservation in their demeanor.

Oddly, he noticed that Sarah was even more reserved around her parents than he was. Sami knew she was gay, but suspected it was not acknowledged openly by her family. When Joe arrived, Sarah visibly relaxed. The brother and sister appeared to have a bond that excluded their parents. Despite the sibling banter and jibes, the two were comfortable with each other which intrigued Sami.

Joe was friendly towards him, yet watchful. What the hell! He was with FBI. But Sarah openly joked about where he'd parked his camel or kept his harem. Sami realized it was her way of clearing the air, and he responded in kind.

"Pool boy," he joked the next afternoon, as he plopped a cold beer in her lap. Anything else I can do for you madam?"

Sarah blinked up at him, shading her eyes with one

freckled hand. "Sorry Ahab, you're not my type, though you do have good teeth and a yummy chest. Have you ever thought of shaving it?"

Karen laughed and clapped her hands over her ears. "I'm not hearing this. La, la, la... Somebody turn up the music."

Sarah's parents had returned to Washington that morning along with Joe. Sami, Karen and Sarah owned the beach that sunny afternoon and were in high spirits, Sarah because Tricia was on her way to join them, Sami and Karen because it was a break from his rigorous schedule at Emory.

It was pointed that Tricia arrived after the parents had left. Sami suspected it was one of many secrets inhabiting the Miles household. As Tolstoy observed, every unhappy family is unhappy in its own way. And despite the affluent trappings, this was not a happy family. He looked at his beautiful wife, dozing in the slanting afternoon sun. The house loomed behind her, its shadow already creeping towards them along the beach. He said a silent prayer that no secret would ever come between them.

Chapter Fifty Four

Duck, NC

Karen saw a figure cross in front of the window. The front door opened. She squinted against the light that shone behind the man standing in the doorway. His face was shadowed but she recognized the coppery glint of his hair. Switching off the ignition, she collected her purse, opened the car door and slid out. The car beeped twice as she pressed the lock button. It struck her as a silly gesture but she realized it was just habit.

She paused a moment leaning against the car. Her legs were wobbly after sitting so long, and she felt light-headed. Walking across the sand-swept drive and up to the house was like moving in a dream with the wind pulling at her hair and her clothes. Joe descended the wooden staircase halfway to meet her. He put his arm around her, helped her up the remaining steps.

Closing the door behind them, he stepped back and looked at Karen. Her face was pale and dark circles ringed the amazing eyes which shimmered now with unshed tears. "I'm so sorry," she whispered before her voice broke. She covered her face as he put his arms around her.

"I know," he said, his own voice hoarse with restrained emotion. "Me too." They clung to each other, two people who were barely familiar, yet joined now in grief. She finally stepped back and pulled a tissue from her pocket.

"I need to use the restroom," she said, keeping her eyes down.

"You remember where it is?" he asked, though it was

more a statement than a question. She nodded, blowing her nose into the tissue.

The cold water on her face revived her. Glancing at the mirror as she dried her hands on a linen towel, she caught the reflection of a small painting on the opposite wall. She knew it was Sarah's even without seeing the signature. It was different from the ones Karen had seen in her loft, but the use of color and composition were familiar. She sensed her friend's presence all around her. When she opened the door, she could imagine Sarah standing there, hands on her hips.

Joe turned from the wet bar as she entered the den. "I'm fixing you something to drink," he said. She dropped into a faded floral overstuffed chair beside the desk and looked around the room. It was as she recalled. The walls were paneled with weathered boards. Antique furniture displayed years of living by the beach. Books lined one wall, best sellers interspersed with classics and one section, near the bottom, which held a well-worn selection of children's favorites. "Mira would love these," she knew and immediately pushed the thought to the back of her mind. She had to remain focused if she was to survive this nightmare. And she must survive.

She watched Joe as he poured a dram of brandy into a small crystal glass. His movements were graceful and economical. She accepted the glass without comment when he handed it to her. "This will help," he said, "but sip it slowly. Have you had anything to eat?"

She nodded. "Yes, I had some soup at a truck stop a few hours ago." Taking a small sip of brandy, she let the warmth flow down through her core. "I'll be okay," she added. Tension was still etched across her face, but her eyes were dry and clear now. She watched as Joe selected a bottle of water for himself. "I need to keep a clear head."

His face was a bit narrow to be called handsome, but it was arresting, like Sarah's had been. The brown eyes regarding her from behind his steel-rimmed glasses were softer than his sister's had been, though just as intelligent.

Karen took another sip and set down her glass. "That would be a good idea for us both," she replied.

"Karen is no bimbo," Sarah had told him. Joe would agree with that.

"I don't have any information from Savannah yet. Are you certain you know who the people are who, who…" he broke off, looking down at the childhood photo of Sarah he had left on the desk. He turned it over.

"All I know is that they threatened my husband. I don't know how many there are. I met one in Sami's office, and he frightened me. If evil has a face, it would be his."

"Sami admitted that he was being threatened?" asked Joe, eyebrows raised. "When?"

She looked down at her hands. "I spoke with him a few hours ago. I had to know he was all right."

"Did you tell him where you were going?" Joe demanded, alarm bells going off in his head. The look on her face gave him the answer.

He pushed up his glasses, put his hand over his eyes and groaned.

"He is not involved," she countered.

"It doesn't matter Karen," he said evenly. "If they tracked you, they can track him."

"I didn't think… I… Oh God." She slumped forward and dropped her head in her hands.

He picked up his Blackberry and was punching in a number when they saw headlight beams trace across the far wall and heard a car come to a stop outside.

Joe pocketed his phone, and ran for the front room with Karen in tow. He stopped beside a window and pulled Karen over next to him. They watched as the lights were extinguished, and Sami exited the car.

Karen gave a small cry. Joe released her, though he remained beside the window, scanning Swallow Lane that led back to Duck road.

* * *

Sami was halfway up the walk when Karen burst through the front door and flew down the steps. His embrace was so tight she held her breath while he buried his face in her hair. He was murmuring in Arabic, endearments she half understood. Then he turned her face up and kissed her cheeks and forehead and lips.

Joe hurried past them and then squatted down in back of Sami's car. Switching on a flashlight, he inspected underneath the back bumper, frowning. Then he slid underneath as Karen and Sami watched. After a few seconds he emerged holding the small tracking device in his hand.

"What?" Sami began but Joe was already speed dialing on his Blackberry. "Lois, I am going to need that backup unit," he said, and then listened intently.

"The doctor just arrived," he continued. "I found a tracking device on his car."

Sami looked down and put a hand to his forehead.

Joe turned to him, all softness gone from his eyes. "I have a swat team on the way, but they may not arrive in time. Do you have any idea how much of a lead you had."

Sami shook his head, too dazed to respond.

Joe looked down at the device in his hand, thinking. Then he looked at Sami and said, "Pull your car around to the garage, I'll open the door. Karen, come with me."

Joe spun back towards the house and Karen followed him up the steps, taking them two at a time. After jabbing the garage door opener, Joe headed for the master bedroom with Karen on his heels. Pulling open the door to the walk-in closet, he fingered a set of keys from his pocket.

"As I recall, you know how to shoot," he said with a knowing look as he opened the gun safe in the corner of the closet.

"Yes," she replied, the hairs beginning to stand up on her arms. "I've shot skeet and trap," she hesitated, "but I've never shot a person."

"Neither have I," he replied, meeting her eyes. "Let's hope it stays that way." He handed her the Browning 20 gauge. It was familiar in her hands. "You used these before when you were here," said Joe. "As I recall, Sami can shoot."

"Yes, he shoots with Dad and me." Karen said as her husband entered the room. Joe held a twin of Karen's shotgun out to Sami who accepted it without a word.

"Here," said Joe, handing them two shells each. "Load these." He watched Sami load his weapon and snap on the safety while Karen followed suit. Then he handed them each additional shells for their pockets. "This is only bird shot, but it will do the job," he instructed. "Just don't let the bastards get too close."

Looking at their faces he added, "The guns are just a precaution. Hopefully you won't need them." Sami and Karen exchanged glances and followed Joe into the den.

"Here's the plan," said Joe. "I need to get rid of this," he pulled the tracking device from his pocket. "I'll lead them away from this house. Sami noticed he had a smaller handgun tucked in his waistband.

"Sami, you watch the front. Karen, you watch the back from the mudroom. And keep the lights out," he said switching off the desk lamp. They both nodded and took their positions.

Joe paused at the front door and looked at Sami. "I'll be back in twenty minutes," he said. "Don't shoot me."

Then he was gone.

Chapter Fifty Five

"This is nuts," thought Joe as he sped along Duck Road. "I don't even know who I'm fighting here. Shit! I don't even know if Sami is telling the truth."

Dawn was etching slivers of light on the horizon, and he wondered if that would be good or bad. When he reached the Sanderling Resort on his left, he pulled into the driveway. The three two-story buildings were mostly dark except for security spotlights creating haloes of illumination. Cars were scattered across the parking lot helter-skelter. The tourist season was nearly at an end.

Joe drove around the back of one building and searched for the service entrance. Rolling down his window, he tossed the tracking device into a dumpster huddled behind the first building. He hoped it would buy them a little time.

He circled back to the road and slammed the Porsche into third gear. Dark forms on either side of him morphed into houses as the night retreated. Joe squinted when he spotted twin pinpricks of light hovering above the empty road ahead. He instinctively decreased his speed a notch, watching the headlights grow. As they drew closer, he realized there was another vehicle behind the first. Both were dark sedans.

Glancing in his rear-view mirror after they passed, Joe noted the Georgia license plate. His stomach flip-flopped, and he said a fervent prayer that he was overreacting. Punching in the number on his car phone, he received an answer on the first ring.

"Where's the team?" he asked.

"On their way," was the response. "Should be there in 35 to 40 minutes. Any updates?"

"Yeah, I think the bad guys just passed me on Duck Road. I diverted them for a while, but I don't know for how long. I'll keep you posted."

Joe waited until the tail lights were no longer visible in his mirror before turning onto Norwood. Swerving around to the side drive of the beach house, he pushed the automatic door opener and eased into the garage. Sami appeared in the doorway from the house as Joe shut off the engine.

"I need you to help me," Joe said as he jumped out of his car and hurried over to a long wooden tool bench half hidden in the corner. Joe switched on a flashlight and pulled over a large dusty waterproof box. He swore under his breath as he sifted through a tangle of tools including wrenches, screwdrivers and pliers.

"Get the key for Karen's car and drive it around to the side here," he called over his shoulder. "Park in the driveway just in front of the garage door.

"All right," Sami responded, already turning back towards the house.

"Tell her to keep watch at the front," Joe added. "I'll explain while we work."

When Sami returned, he saw Joe unscrewing the license plate on his Porsche. He pocketed the key fob as he slammed the car door and hurried over to Joe. Tossing a second screwdriver to Sami, Joe instructed him to remove the plate on the Mercedes."

"Do you have any idea what kind of car these guys would be driving?" Joe asked as he exchanged his Washington, DC plate for the Georgia plate Sami had just pulled off the big car.

Sami glanced up before fitting in the first screw and

twisting. "No, I've only met one of them and never saw a car. Why?"

"Two dark sedans passed me on my way back. They gave me a bad feeling."

Sami paused for a moment, before continuing with his task. "They would know I stopped somewhere for a while," he said as he turned the final screw. Pushing back up to his feet, he handed Joe the license plate and looked from him to the Porsche. "When they realize they have been tricked, they might remember passing your car. I would."

Joe nodded. "That is a disadvantage with a sports car. Come on, let's get inside and talk this out." He punched the button that brought the automatic door rumbling down and thanked the fates that the garage had no windows.

Chapter Fifty Six

Abdullah and Mahmoud stood next to the dumpster and scanned the area behind the resort.

The driver's door of Khalid's car burst open, and he exploded from the vehicle. "Well?" he demanded.

Mahmoud shrugged, "It must be in there," he said, pointing to the giant metal receptacle. He was tall enough to peek over the top and see that it was full. He wrinkled his nose at the smell of garbage. It was not an overwhelming odor like in the Middle East, but all the same, he had no desire to dig through it.

"How did he discover the device?" asked Abdullah.

Khalid turned and stared at him until Abdullah looked down.

"He is with his wife," said Khalid, struggling to control his voice. "She was warned and now they are both here with someone helping them. What other explanation is there?"

Neither of his companions answered.

A gray metal door opened, and a large man stepped outside into the pool of light from an overhead fixture. A stained apron stretched across his paunch, and the shadow of a beard grizzled his cheeks and chin. He bent to light a cigarette, then tossed the match and looked up catching sight of the three men.

His eyes widened and then narrowed. He blew out a cloud of smoke, "Can I help you find something?" he asked.

"No," said Khalid, "we are looking to check in and must have taken the wrong drive."

The man studied them and then jerked his thumb to the left. "You need to go back around that way to the front," he growled.

Mahmoud glanced at Khalid. "He will remember our faces," he said under his breath in Arabic as he watched the man take a step backward towards the door behind him.

"It won't matter," replied Khalid and then smiled at the man. "Thank you sir, we will do as you say," he said in English.

Back in their car, Abdullah and Mahmoud followed Khalid to the front of the resort. Mahmoud looked up at the rear-view mirror and saw the man still watching them. He didn't like it. "It feels wrong leaving him alive as a witness. He knows our faces and our cars. Khalid is growing careless," he said to Abdullah.

His partner was searching the glove box for antacids. "Khalid is in charge," was Abdullah's patent reply. "We must obey his orders."

Khalid pulled into a space at the far corner of the parking lot in front of the last building. Mahmoud eased in next to him and lowered his window.

Khalid gestured for a cigarette. Mahmoud drew out a butt and then tossed the pack to him. Abdullah sighed and lowered his own window.

Khalid's face hung like a floating death's head in the predawn light. His eyes burned like coals in the hollow orbs of their sockets. He had to will his hand to be steady as he struck a match and lit the cigarette. Inhaling deeply, he closed his eyes and leaned his head back before exhaling.

"The device showed the doctor was stopped somewhere for about fifteen minutes, said Khalid. "Someone warned him about the tracking device, possibly the wife. It was removed and thrown away here to mislead us."

Khalid opened his eyes and studied the burning ember on the tip of his cigarette. Then he looked up at the road. "He may have continued on."

"I don't think so," Mahmoud said slowly, looking back toward the direction from which they came. "Do you remember the car we passed on the way here?"

Khalid's eyes flickered.

"Yes," replied Abdullah, recalling the sleek silver sports car. Only the sons of sheiks possessed such things in his world.

"You may be right," said Khalid. "We will go back to that location and begin searching. We are looking for the silver car or any cars with plates from Hilton Head or Atlanta. If you find anything, call me and I will do the same."

They all agreed and Mahmoud took one last pull on his cigarette before tossing it out the window and cranking the engine.

"They are close," said Khalid, discarding his own smoke. "I can feel it. With Allah's guidance we will find them. And they will pay."

Chapter Fifty Seven

Joe selected a shotgun for himself and was checking his ammo. The Glock Pistol was still tucked in his waistband. Joining Sami at the front window, he scanned the landscape. The sun had just risen but hid behind the clouds. A heavy mist had rolled in from the ocean and obliterated the road.

"Your wife described the man who came to your office," said Joe. "Was he the only contact you had?"

"No," replied Sami. "I was first contacted by phone. The caller told me I would be visited by a messenger. His accent was Egyptian."

Joe's eyebrows rose. "Al Jihad?"

"I wouldn't know," quipped Sami. "I am not an expert on terrorist groups."

Joe nodded but kept his eyes on the window. "Do you think you would recognize the voice?"

"Yes, I have a copy of it. I record all calls that come in on my office phone."

Joe turned to stare at him. "What do they want from you?"

"Something I can't give them," Sami replied, weary of repeating the story. "They believe a CDC shipment will be going to Dugway for disposal. They want me to provide the date and time."

"Christ! And you tried to handle it on your own?"

"I reported it to my superior who assured me he would take care of it." Sami looked away. "I was a fool. I know it doesn't help, but I'll never forgive myself for Sarah...for all of this."

Joe bit his lower lip. "You're not the bad guy here," he said, turning away and glancing toward the back of the house. "I'm going to check on Karen."

"Wait," said Sami. "Did you see that?"

"What?" said Joe, instantly alert as he rejoined Sami beside the window.

"Over there," Sami raised his chin toward the right side of the property. I thought I saw movement behind the fog, but I couldn't make it out."

They stared at the spot for thirty seconds before Joe spoke. "Close the action on your gun and be ready. I'm going upstairs to see if I can get a better view."

Sami snapped the action in place. "Have you done this before?" he asked, regarding the other man with narrowed eyes.

"In training exercises," Joe replied. "I'm not exactly a field agent, but I know what to do." He thought of Sarah's frequent jibes and winced.

"If we're lucky, the team will get here first. Call me if you see any movement at all." Joe gave Sami a tight smile which the other man returned.

Whistling in the dark, thought Joe, heading up the stairs.

Chapter Fifty Eight

Norfolk, VA

"Goddamn you Joe!" thought Lois, as she pulled on her gear. "What are you trying to prove?" She had read the report from Savannah. These were very bad people. It frustrated her to be operating blind like this. Not only was she in the dark about who these guys were, she had no idea how many there were. At least the doctor's wife should be able to ID one of them — if they got to her in time.

That was precisely what she'd had to explain to convince her director, Walt Broomfield. "I know Charlotte has jurisdiction in North Carolina, but Norfolk is only 55 miles from Duck. If we have to deploy, we'll need to get there ASAP."

"You know I'm not comfortable with this," Walt replied. He'd left home to meet her at his office around midnight and was dressed casually in well worn chinos and a sport coat. He was probably in his early fifties but still fit and attractive with just enough gray at the temples to add gravitas.

"I don't like the loose ends," he continued, "undocumented terrorists, the wife fleeing a murder scene, and the Palestinian doctor God knows where."

"I understand sir. But these situations seldom follow the textbook…"

"Don't lecture me," he growled, slapping his desk. Then he pointed a finger. "I'm only doing this for you. Do you understand?"

"Yes sir, I appreciate that." Lois attempted a smile.

He leaned back in his chair and ran his tongue across

his front teeth as he regarded her. "You said Agent Miles called you. How well do you know him?"

"We were at the academy together," said Lois. "This is the first time I've heard from him since then." She kept her eyes locked on his.

"Personal feelings can sometimes generate bad decisions. I'm trusting you on this Castellari. Don't fuck it up."

"No sir." She fought to keep her face impassive. She'd won.

Chapter Fifty Nine

Duck, NC

The fog amplified the difficulty of their search. Abdullah especially was spooked. He had endured sandstorms that didn't make him feel half as vulnerable as this evil mist that enveloped them. Smoky tendrils floated and swirled like the jinn devils that inhabited nightmares. The infidel woman's paintings flashed before him, and he rubbed his eyes to banish the images. He fingered the prayer beads in his pocket.

Khalid had timed the distance from the resort to the place where the silver car passed them. He compared it to the time span when the tracking device most recently started and stopped. It matched. If Mahmoud's prediction was correct, they were very close. Khalid turned onto Pelican Road. Abdullah and Mahmoud turned onto Norwood. Both roads led to Swallow Lane.

Leaning forward, Mahmoud squinted at the windshield. "I see a car," he said, pointing to the elusive form of a house in front of them. Abdullah looked and saw it too, just before a cloud drifted across the drive to swallow it.

Easing his car behind a dune topped with clumps of scrub and sea oats, Mahmoud killed the lights. "I'll check the plates on the car and survey the house," he said, pulling his weapon and checking the silencer. "You keep watch and alert me if you see anything." He thumbed his phone to the vibrate setting.

Training from the camps in Yemen kicked in as Mahmoud made a crouching run towards the parked auto. A rush of adrenaline surged through his body and heightened his senses.

Noting the Atlanta license plate, he rose to peek in the rear window of the car, when a shrill yelp split the night. The door to the beach house opened and Mahmoud ducked behind the vehicle as a woman stepped out on the porch. A small, rat-like dog spun down the steps and headed directly for Mahmoud.

He gestured with his gun as though to strike the animal. It jumped back but then held its ground and hunkered down while baring tiny needle teeth in a growl. He wanted to kill the filthy beast but knew better. The woman had come to the head of the steps and was peering into the fog.

"Shaki? What is it? Have you cornered a possum again?"

She came down two steps and then hesitated. Mahmoud held his silenced gun ready for three shots, one in the head and one in the heart. Then one for the beast.

The woman appeared hazy in the mist, but he could tell from her voice she was not young. Light pouring from the doorway illuminated a tousled mop of yellow hair and a pink terrycloth robe. She appeared unwilling to venture into the shrouded yard, and grasping the banister she called again to the dog.

"Shakirius! I mean it, you come here now!"

The dog apparently took this as a sign she meant business. With a final growl and series of yips, he scampered back to his mistress. She scooped up the animal, murmuring as she carried it back inside.

Mahmoud lowered his gun. This was not the house.

* * *

The fog was lifting and Mahmoud was growing anxious. Their cover would soon be gone, and he would have to approach the houses in full daylight. When he reached Swallow Lane, he looked both ways. To the right, he saw two houses. Both were large and erected on pilings. The house closest to them appeared shuttered and vacant.

Mahmoud nosed into the driveway. Putting his car in park, he studied the neighboring house on the end. It was partially hidden by scrub which was good. A series of small windows located high up lined the side of the house. He supposed them to be for a bathroom or bedrooms. Through breaks in the fog, he could see the second story windows were curtained but not shuttered.

"I'm going to approach from this side," said Mahmoud. "You cover me from behind the scrub."

Abdullah nodded. He had spoken very little in the past half hour, and Mahmoud could see pain and fear etched on his narrow face.

"We trained for this together, brother," he continued, clasping Abdullah's sinewy shoulder in his large hand. "The end is near and our glory close at hand. *Allahu akbar!*"

"*Allahu akbar!*" Abdullah affirmed, though his eyes remained haunted as the two men exited the sedan. Crouching behind the scrub, he watched as Mahmoud darted across the open space to the side of the neighboring house and then disappeared in the pilings underneath.

Holding his breath, Mahmoud waited for several seconds. The area beneath the house was dark and dank from the sea mist. He picked out the shadowy forms of several small canoes and a pile of buoys atop a clump of netting. Hearing nothing, he continued. The fog was creeping back. It would not be good for Abdullah as his backup, but it served Mahmoud's purpose well.

He shoved his gun into his waistband and got down on hands and knees. Inching forward through the damp sand, he sought to make no sound. When he finally reached the far side, he chanced a peek to the front of the house. He would not be visible from the windows there. Pulling out his gun, he rose and flattened himself against the side of the garage.

Moving slowly, he paused at the corner and made a hand gesture, not sure if Abdullah would see him. He braced himself with a two-handed gun hold and leapt around the side of the structure.

He quickly determined that he was alone and crouched down next to the car parked in front of the garage. He recognized it as a Mercedes. It was gold and a fairly new model, maybe two years old. It was the type of car he had seen at the embarkation center in Hilton Head. He slid his fingers alongside the hood. It was warm.

Crawling to the back of the vehicle, he read the license plate: Washington, DC. He touched it and noticed that a bottom screw was loose. Raising himself a little, he inspected the rear window. He smiled when he recognized the small circular decal on the bottom left of the window. It displayed a palm tree with a crescent moon and read: Hilton Head Island. Crouching back down, he slipped out his cell and speed-dialed Khalid's number.

* * *

Abdullah was breathing in ragged gulps. The heavy air constricted his lungs and made his heart race. Mahmoud said he would signal back, but he had not seen him since he vanished beneath the house. Now he could barely see the house. What should he do? Call Khalid? Follow Mahmoud? He pulled out his cell and stared with dismay at the blank screen. He couldn't remember when he had last plugged it into the car charger.

He fingered his prayer beads and said a silent prayer to Allah for guidance before cocking his gun and following the wall of scrub to the back. He pushed through a break in the bushes and dashed for the pilings .The space was higher than in front, and he felt vulnerable though he knew he was invisible from the house. He couldn't see the ocean but could hear its relentless surf roaring in and sucking back out. Several yards in front of him, he could make out the swimming pool surrounded by lounge chairs and tables. He gave it a wide berth and crept on until he reached a flight of stairs leading to the back deck. Should he wait for Mahmoud or continue forward and meet him on the other side?

Chapter Sixty

Karen rubbed her eyes, gritty from straining to see through the fog. It seemed to be growing worse again. Shifting the Browning, she caught a glimpse of movement along the side of the pool. She blinked and then squinted at the spot.

Karen snapped the barrel of her shotgun into place and waited until she heard a creak at the bottom of the steps outside. She eased open the mudroom door a crack and was startled to see Abdullah peering up the back staircase. He saw her at the same instant.

She registered the surprise on his face. On instinct, Karen kicked the door open with her foot. Fingering the trigger, Karen heard her father's words, "Don't aim, just point and shoot. Abdullah had recovered and was raising his pistol.

Boom! Boom! The shots reverberated back through the silent house.

Sami ran across the front room and down the hall to the back of the house. "Karen!" he shouted. The back door stood open with mist creeping in and pooling along the wood floor.

Raising his shotgun, Sami stepped outside where he saw Karen standing at the bottom of the staircase. She held her gun as if ready to fire again and was staring at a man's body which lay crumpled in the sand at her feet. A stain of red was expanding across the victim's chest. His lifeless eyes stared up at the gray sky. Sami took the steps two at a time to join her.

A piercing scream rent the morning air, and Sami and Karen looked up in horror as Khalid came charging towards them from the far end of the pool. His face was distorted with rage, and he stopped short when he saw the gun in Karen's hands.

"Filthy whore!" he screamed and with a steady stream of curses he raised his own weapon and began shooting wildly.

Sami shoved Karen behind him and raised his own shotgun.

Boom!

The first shot grazed Khalid's shoulder, spinning him around.

Boom!

The second shot hit him full in the face. His body reeled and plunged backwards into the pool.

"Sami!" Karen had thrown down her gun and reached out towards her husband. He looked back. Dropping his own weapon he staggered and fell into her arms. He clutched his left side, and when his hand came away, it was bright red.

"It's okay," she murmured, cradling her husband. "It's going to be okay. We'll get you to a hospital." She pressed her hand down tight on top of his to staunch the bleeding. "My love, my love."

As if in a dream, Karen saw the third man approach. He was big with a wide handsome face that was strangely devoid of emotion. His weapon hung at his side as he surveyed the scene. Abdullah's body in a heap at the foot of the stairs, Khalid's floating face down in the pool.

The woman looked up at him, as she held her husband against her breasts. Dark hair swirled around her tear-streaked face. He raised his gun to point at her forehead. She didn't move. Her eyes glittered, green as an oasis.

The distant whirring which none of them had registered, suddenly became deafening as a helicopter roared over the house and then hovered above the beach.

Mahmoud looked up and said a silent prayer. A moment

later, first one, and then a second load of birdshot tore through his upper body. Joe advanced steadily towards him. He threw down the shotgun, pulled out his Glock and fired until the chamber was empty.

"FBI!" someone boomed over a loud speaker. "Throw down your weapons!"

The lights of the chopper cut through the retreating fog and illuminated the scene. Joe hurried towards them holding his gun in one raised hand and his badge in the other. His blue FBI jacket billowed out behind him.

"I'm FBI," he yelled over the whap, whap of the chopper. "I need an ambulance!"

The team ducked low to avoid the blades as they ran towards him. Joe saw a stretcher being unloaded and prayed it would be in time. He glanced behind him at Karen, whose hand was still pressed to her husband's side. Sami's eyes were closed.

"Help him," she screamed. "Someone please help him!"

Chapter Sixty One

Decatur, GA
September, 2010

The Teacher stands unprotected on the hilltop, pulling the hood of his slicker down further to protect his face from the steady drizzle. He can just make out the coffin being lowered into the ground.

Three men for one. The mission aborted. No matter, the men were fools and have been redeemed now as martyrs. There will be other missions, thanks to the endless source of money pouring out of Saudi Arabia. This could even serve as a lesson. Let those who have strayed from Islam see what happens to traitors and infidels.

As he turns to leave, he startles at the sight of three men walking towards him. They all wear blue jackets. He reaches into the pocket of his slicker.

"FBI," the lead man shouts. "Put your hands in the air!"

Each man has a weapon trained at his head. The one in the middle holds up a badge. He stops a few feet in front of The Teacher and looks him directly in the eye. "Give me an excuse," he says softly. He is bare-headed and rain droplets cling to his short coppery hair and eyelashes.

The Teacher slowly withdraws his hand. Smiling, he raises both hands in the air. "You have nothing on me," he replies in his Oxford English. "You will regret this harassment of an innocent man."

"Why are you here?" Joe asks.

"My lawyer will explain."

"Yes, he will have a lot to explain about Dr. Sami Nasser."

"Dead men don't talk," The Teacher sneers.

"Maybe so, but very clever men record their phone calls," Joe answers, and watches with satisfaction as the smile fades from The Teacher's face.

* * *

The lights are dim in the ICU in Sentara Norfolk General Hospital. Sami's eyelashes flutter. His head aches and he vaguely recalls some chaotic scene of violence and an urgent need to act. He wonders if he is dreaming. But there is no pain in dreams. He opens his eyes and waits for them to focus.

The room smells of antiseptic, and he is intimate with that smell. The hushed voices, the low lights, the bleeping machines, they are all familiar and comforting.

His eyes rest on a piece of paper taped to the railing of his metal bed. He squints and makes out a crayon drawing of a yellow sun shining over a scribble of green grass and a lopsided brown tree. Three stick figures are holding hands and smiling with the smallest in the middle. "I LOVE YOU DADDY" is scrawled in wobbly block letters across the top of the page, and "MIRA" at the bottom.

A warm hand cups his own, and he looks down to see slender fingers laced with his and a tousled dark head beside them.

He grimaces with the effort to move his hand and touch the hair, so soft.

The head slowly raises and he watches as tears slide down the most beautiful face in the world.

"*Habibti,*" he whispers.

Epilog

Duck, NC

Joe leans against the railing of his beach house and gazes out over the ocean as he sips his bourbon. The blood has been scrubbed away, the pool cleaned. The real estate woman had tactfully avoided any questions regarding the recent history of the house. He is glad she left. After a morning of being grilled by his superiors at the bureau, he needs time to recuperate.

The fake funeral had been his idea and not very well received at first. Computer geeks are not the top of the food chain in the organization, but he had earned his right to speak. Lois's support had been the final straw that tipped the decision in his favor.

She comes up behind him now, circling his waist and pressing her face against his shoulder.

"Why were you so sure The Teacher would make an appearance?" she asks.

He pauses, running his free hand along her arm. "To be honest, I wasn't." Sami had told him about the mysterious phone call that set the whole episode in motion. The caller was obviously educated and certainly no fool. But even crafty men make mistakes, especially when ego is involved.

"If you'd been wrong it would have been my ass," she grouses.

"But I was right," he smiles. "And if we hadn't tried, maybe the next plot would be successful. Eventually that will happen, but I don't want it to be on our watch."

Joe sets his drink on the porch rail, stretches and yawns.

"I wonder what Sarah would think?" he muses. "Should her geeky old brother become a field agent?"

The wind whips across the beach, making little wavelets on the pool below. It blows sand across the gray wood slats beneath their bare feet. A squadron of pelicans skims low above the dense blue ocean, the birds' powerful wings spread motionless.

Lois steps up to the railing beside Joe, linking her arm in his. Her laugh echoes in the wind. "Hell yes."

CPSIA information can be obtained at www.ICGtesting.com
Printed in the USA
LVOW122212050212

267200LV00001B/1/P